Six Thousand Miles

Six
Thousand
Miles

T. MALONE

This is the raw, captivating story of one woman's journey of discovering and fulfilling her mind, body, and soul. Six thousand miles lie between the woman she is, the woman she becomes, and the man that changed it all forever.

ARCHWAY
PUBLISHING

Archway Publishing books may be ordered through booksellers or by contacting:

Archway Publishing
1663 Liberty Drive
Bloomington, IN 47403
www.archwaypublishing.com
1 (888) 242-5904

Because of the dynamic nature of the Internet, any web addresses or
links contained in this book may have changed since publication and
may no longer be valid. The views expressed in this work are solely those
of the author and do not necessarily reflect the views of the publisher,
and the publisher hereby disclaims any responsibility for them.

Any people depicted in stock imagery provided by Thinkstock are models,
and such images are being used for illustrative purposes only.
Certain stock imagery © Thinkstock.

ISBN: 978-1-4808-2082-1 (sc)
ISBN: 978-1-4808-1438-7 (hc)
ISBN: 978-1-4808-1439-4 (e)

Library of Congress Control Number: 2015913311

Print information available on the last page.

Archway Publishing rev. date: 10/28/2015

CONTENTS

CHAPTER 1

Displaced in New York

My head was full of busyness—*chitter, chatter, chitter, chatter*—not just that afternoon but every minute of every afternoon.

Sometimes I wondered how I remembered anything. I swear, if it wasn't for my smartphone calling me a dummy, I never would have remembered a thing. I often thought that I was the only person who was honest enough—no, scratch that, dumb enough—to admit that without technology I wouldn't remember to wake up in the morning.

Maybe it was only that bad a few days of the week, or maybe just the days that ended in *y*. I thought there must be a country song to that effect, or maybe there should be a song about the days that I would have rather not woken up. *I hope my files for the scheduled meetings aren't as scattered.*

Suddenly, my thoughts were interrupted as I felt a man standing over me, waiting to take my order.

"Oh shoot, is it my turn to order? I don't know. There is so much on this dang menu. I generally don't drink coffee. I just started for some odd reason. I think because it is cold here in New York, and I am from a tropical climate," I babbled.

"Excuse me, ma'am?" The man stared at me, not understanding what the heck I was talking about.

"I'm looking for anything, really, just to warm my bones. Coffee shops seem to be everywhere you go here." I was having a conversation with myself.

The man started to back away. He probably thought I was crazy.

"Okay, yes, yes! Come back. I'll just have a normal cup of coffee, black coffee." My decision was made.

The man looked at me like I was a sinner in his coffeehouse of saints. He walked away.

"Please. I didn't say I wouldn't tip you!" I said under my breath.

He delivered the coffee quickly. Ah, yes! The warm cup immediately enveloped my hands, instead of the other way around. Was my cup blue? *It should be blue from my cold hands on this frigid, gray day*, I thought. I felt other customers staring at me as I held my cup as if I were praying. Yeah, praying that I was back home.

After I finished my coffee, I went out into the gray, bleak weather again. I was lost in this environment, and the people were always in a hurry here. I wondered if they could see how lost I was, if they could see how cold I was. I pulled my coat tightly around myself and buried my mouth in the upturned collar. I started to daydream.

I remembered the warm sand beneath my toes. As I lost track of my surroundings, I looked up and imagined the blue sky meeting the horizon at sunset. With a screech of tires and a honking of horns, I was forced back to the cold reality. I jumped back onto the footpath.

"Sorry, I didn't see you!" I yelled at the top of my voice, but the car was long gone. *What's his hurry? Jeez, one honk would have been sufficient—okay, maybe two*, I thought. "C'mon, do you even know or care how far out of my element I am at this point? I don't even know," I muttered under my breath, feeling a little shaken up. Back home we didn't honk horns! It was considered quit rude! Like I needed another reason to hate it here.

It was only 3:39 p.m., and it was already getting dark. Walking up the dead street to my quiet hotel, I was shivering. I consoled myself by remembering I would be calling home to get a taste of Hawaii and catch up with my girls every night. How had I ended up here anyway? Oh, yes, I wanted to take on the world! I had this grand idea of being Ms. Business Tycoon. I would start a world-class retail store and spa featuring herbal products that no one could turn down. Living in Hawaii, I had learned about the benefits of such products. I would give the public something different—change the commercial approach to the business and have customers feel as if their warm, functioning bodies were in a tropical climate! They could live a longer, fuller life. I would achieve an award for businesswoman of the year, three years running!

I would do all this, of course, while continuing my top-performing construction company in Maui with my partner there, and when the time was right, I would sell out my share. I couldn't rethink that dream now. *Time to forge on, young—or middle-aged one*, I told myself. I believed in this; I couldn't go wrong.

⊱┈⟡┈◯┈⟡┈⊰

The next day, I was faced with reports, phone calls, fires to put out, and a meeting to prep for. Sounded like a great Friday night. But it wasn't like I ever had Friday nights anyway. I dared to wonder what that would be like. I wondered what it was like to be longed for, kissed in the moonlight like in the lyrics of a song.

I had to get my mind back on work and stop daydreaming about fairy tales! I had a construction crew waiting for my phone call in the dawn hours on a job site on Kauai. Then I had to prepare for meetings regarding the spa. I quickly called my contracting partner in Hawaii, who assured me everything was going according to schedule. When he asked how I was, I abruptly ended the conversation. I didn't want him knowing how stressed I had become; the last thing I needed now was a concerned partner in Hawaii. I spent the rest of my day preparing for my meeting the next morning with the only prospect I had found for taking over the spa. We were scheduled to meet at nine o'clock in the hotel lobby.

⊱┈⟡┈◯┈⟡┈⊰

I walked down to the lobby the next morning, and standing by the door was a burly character wearing a heavy wool coat that hung down to his calves. I walked over to him.

"Mr. Snow, good morning. I'm Tia Malone." I extended my hand. "It is good to meet with you in person. I have a lot to talk to you about," I said eagerly.

"Good morning, Ms. Malone." He shook my hand gently.

Why can't a man give a woman a firm handshake? I wondered. "Let's sit at that table," I said, pointing. "It's closest to the fireplace; it'll be a lot warmer."

He hesitated and looked preoccupied. "Sorry, Ms. Malone, I can't stay. I've been called away." He turned to the doorman. "Please get me a cab?"

"But I thought we were going to have a meeting. Are you not interested in taking over the business?"

"Ms. Malone, this isn't about you. I have a personal emergency and will call you in a few days," he said abruptly.

I wondered whether he hadn't prepped, or maybe at first glance, I just hadn't impressed him. Either way, I certainly wasn't encouraged by the outcome.

After he left, I pulled on my coat and wrapped my long scarf three times around my neck just like I had witnessed others doing, ready to head to the spa for a long day's work. I walked at a good pace to keep warm, feeling doubtful that Mr. Snow was interested in buying out Herbal Essence Longevity, Inc. Maybe I had read too much into our previous discussions. This was really too bad. I had been looking forward to settling this that day. I decided not to rule him out completely just yet. He may have been legit.

>─┤◄›─○─‹►┤─◄

Weeks earlier, when my spa partner in upstate New York called, explaining the personal issues that had come up for him, I had begun pointing out the legalities of our contract. I had reminded him that we were partners, and he couldn't just walk away.

Or could he? What's stopping him? I thought. "No, no, no, you have alternatives," I said, trying to explain.

Have you ever tried explaining why strawberries are red and not blue to a four-year-old who wants to color them blue? That was the kind of situation I was dealing with. One alternative is to give the blue crayon and let judgment come via any means. But you still need be there to say how gorgeous you think the blue strawberries are to keep up the motivation. That will last only so long, though; soon there will be fallout, after everyone else has babied him through the blue-strawberry phase. Then there you are, by yourself, scrubbing out the stains.

Such was business. I was responsible for scrubbing up those stains my partner had left by walking away! Now I had to find out what was happening in the business myself. Was it a staff issue or a training issue, or was the problem stemming from my partner?

On dragged my dreary days and my daily stop to warm myself with a hot coffee. I found that I had actually begun to like the coffee guy. By the time I would get to the third block in on the hike from my hotel to the spa, my lungs would hurt from being so cold. Okay, maybe that was stretching things. The cold did take my breath away, though, and I was happy when the coffee guy would place my coffee in front of me. I had become a regular. I didn't even have to order, and that somehow made me feel very special.

⊱—⊰⊹⊰—◯—⊱⊹⊱—⊰

My meeting on this day was with the one and only Mr. Boss. When I arrived at his office and learned that he was out on the golf course, I thought I would have to find my way to the course by myself, but his assistant had been dragged into the task of getting me there.

I regretfully told him about my one prospect, how my partner had walked away, and what my plans were for finding a good manager to run things while I tried to sell an operating spa. I asked for his help for three months. He was only half-listening until I gave him my ideas. Wow! Mr. Boss became much more interested in my little pitch this time. The meeting clicked along, and I recommitted to the name I had given him. "Mr. Boss" was suitable for him because he was bossy, or maybe it was the way he stated what he wanted. Maybe I needed to be more like that.

He asked me if I would like to go warm up with a cup of coffee. I thought that was a great idea. *Hmm, now I can get to know you a little better*, I thought.

We took our seats in a booth by the windows. The seats were red and warm to the touch from the sun beaming in. We ordered coffee, and even before we received it, I started asking questions.

"Tell me a little about yourself—may I call you Mike?" I asked.

"Yes, of course. What do you want to know?"

"How about your family? Do you have a big family?"

"Well, I am the oldest of five children. My parents divorced when I was just fourteen, and we were all put into different foster homes," he said, taking a gulp of coffee.

"Mike, I am sorry to hear that. How difficult that must have been."

His demeanor and facial expression had changed, and I suddenly felt guilty for asking. Playing with his coffee spoon, he lowered his eyes.

"Mom couldn't afford to keep us after Dad left. She could only manage to give us a very poor upbringing," he said. He glanced up at me, and the look on his face made my heart miss a beat. I hadn't bargained for this emotional trip. His words resonated with me. "Tia, I remember begging for a sandwich when I was a kid just outside of one of the restaurants I own today," he said, picking up his coffee.

"Mike, you must be kidding," I said foolishly, not knowing what else to say.

"No, I'm serious. Today, I never let anyone go hungry," he stated proudly. "Remember that one time I was talking on the phone with you, and I abruptly told you to hold on?"

"Yes, yes, I heard you yelling at your restaurant manager. You were very angry and told me that you would call me back."

"Good memory, Tia. Well, that night the staff had kicked an old couple out of the restaurant because they couldn't pay for their food. I brought them back in and let them eat all they could. After that incident I instructed my staff to never, under any circumstances, turn anyone away that could not afford to eat."

"That was very kind of you. I guess your memory of going hungry has contributed to concern for others," I said, smiling respectfully. I liked this guy more every time we spoke.

"Yes, my employees are to feed the unfortunate and only take whatever those people can pay. They are to do it the first time and even the second time, but if it happens a third time with the same people, they are to serve them and then call me to come down and take care of things."

"What do you do with these people? You can't feed everyone all the time," I said apprehensively.

"Let's talk about that another time, Tia. I need to get back now."

I quickly took his personal cell number in case there were any loose ends that we needed to tie up. He seemed very hands-on with the paperwork, and I thought we would be able to handle a smooth takeover together, if I found a buyer. I wasn't sure at that point whether it made financial sense, but I was willing to try. I was grateful because I knew if he stepped out completely, my only choice would be a complete shutdown.

When we got back to his office, and the deal was finalized, Mr. Boss offered his aid in any way possible.

Yeah, it's not like I have any other businesses to run! I thought.

Mike was a very busy contractor, business owner, and landlord of numerous commercial properties, not to mention apartment buildings. I considered myself lucky that he happened to be the landlord of the mall in which the spa was located. The property was new, and he needed to keep tenants in 90 percent of the spaces to avoid interruptions with investors and other projects. Keeping the spa from shutting down was in both of our best interests. I was comforted by the knowledge that he would watch over things for three months while I retrained and hired some new staff. Then the plan was that I would visit every few months and work on attracting a buyer. Now I could relax while securing a good team and then head back to my warm home.

My mind had become even busier—and I had become emotional about this project. I never before had been emotional about a business venture. Why now, I wondered. Why this project?

Two weeks later, I had my team in place. I had found a trustworthy manager who came with good references and who had been in the spa business for ten years. I had one more order of business to attend to before I could think about packing for home. I was in deep conversation with a sign contractor, with my back to the front doors of the spa, when a strong arm wrapped gently around my waist, and I heard a familiar strong, gruff voice.

"Now you'll take care of her on the price, Wally, won't ya?" he said. I recognized Mr. Boss's firm tone, even before I smelled his cologne.

"Yes, sir, I will," Wally answered nervously.

Mr. Boss turned to me. "Are you leaving today?"

I nodded my head yes.

"Can I speak to you a moment outside in private?" he asked as he patted my side.

"Of course," I said, turning around. I exited the building behind him and turned to the right of the doorway.

"I think you should know that I think you are beautiful," he said with a smile.

"Well, thank you," I said, puzzled and rather taken aback.

"I just thought I should tell you. I may not get the chance again."

I sensed a bit of nervous energy. Was it coming from him or me? All too soon, he leaned in and kissed me very gently on the lips. He walked to the curb, opened the door of his truck, got in, and waved good-bye before I had even really recovered. To him it was probably just a friendly "you go get 'em, girl; I have faith in you" kind of kiss. But for me there had been electricity when our lips touched. I stood there trying to look like I was sizing up the sign possibilities as he drove off, but I was actually partially dizzy and confused. I wondered, was it that little kiss, or had the sun just come out and warmed up the concrete about ten degrees? Whatever it was, the rest of my day flew by.

CHAPTER 2

Homeward Bound

*A*s I walked through the lobby of the hotel, the desk clerk looked up and asked, "Would you still like a 3:30 a.m. wakeup call, Ms. Malone?"

"Oh yes, please, I have a long day of travel tomorrow. Thank you very much!"

Ugh, I thought. Waking at three thirty in the morning was utterly ridiculous, but I was homeward bound. "Lights out, little missy," I said out loud to myself. "In about thirty hours your head will be lying on a pillow in paradise."

The drive to the airport the next morning was uneventful. When I hit the city, the traffic was nothing less than mind-boggling. There weren't even this many cars in my entire state! It was amazing how adapted I had become to my laid-back life.

"Recalculating," said a familiar voice, interrupting my thoughts.

How can that be? I questioned. *How could a road just end here without any warning?* I thanked God for my GPS. I had nicknamed her Rosie. She was my true robot assistant while I drove, and she said "recalculating" often because I never paid attention to her instructions. I was always thinking of a thousand other things. In true assistant fashion, though, she was persistent!

Rosie got me back on track, and very soon I saw the huge airport, but the exit was to the left, and I was in the right lane. I looked in my rearview mirror and wondered how to get across. I immediately put on my hazard lights and frantically waved my hand out the window, pointing to the exit while I inched my way over. Horns were blaring, and fists and middle fingers were flying, but I had to get in that lane. "Sorry, people," I said aloud. There was no way I was going to miss this flight! Right about then, I missed Mr. Boss. I didn't know what had made me think of him in that moment, but I couldn't daydream right now. It was clear that both Rosie and I needed to pay attention!

I found the car return lot, took my ticket, and parked my car. I managed to get my huge suitcases out without much trouble, placed my keys in the drop box, and headed over to the terminal. I literally couldn't feel my fingers around my suitcase handle because it was heavy, and it was so freaking cold. Packing for a month at a time was just stupid. I really had to do something about that. I made a mental note to pack lighter next time and maybe try a warmer month for travel.

As I struggled to get across the parking lot, I heard more of that familiar New York honking and knew it was meant for me. *Oh my god, people*, I thought, *stop already with the honking.* I hustled across the street as fast as I could in the slush. I glanced down and noticed my shoes were already showing signs that they were not made for this brutal weather. I knew that I should have worn those stupid sneakers and changed at the terminal. I just needed to be home *now*! I felt close to tears.

>—+◆>—◯—<◆+—<

I made it inside, got checked in, and managed to get a window seat. I was so happy to see that big, heavy suitcase disappear behind the ticket agent on its way to my plane. Security was a breeze, and I made it to my gate just as they called for my flight to board.

Finally, I was seated. Island-style music filled the cabin, and flight attendants calmly aided passengers with their belongings. I could smell home in the form of the flower leis the flight attendants were wearing. I could never sleep on planes, but I had promised myself this would still be a good flight, though long. I felt calmer than I had felt in weeks.

I felt the rush of the engine, and the plane accelerated down the runway. Then we had lift-off. I heard the landing gear stow away, and I was on my way home. I almost felt like I was leaving something behind, though I couldn't imagine what on earth that would be, and right then I really didn't care.

>—◦—◦—◦—◦—◦—<

"Aloha, ladies and gentlemen. Welcome to the island of Maui. The local time is 3:30 p.m., and it is a balmy eighty-three degrees. We hope you have a wonderful stay, and *mahalo*—thank you—for flying with us today."

Yeah, I was home! As I crossed the jet bridge, I felt the warmth I hadn't for so long, and it was almost uncomfortable. I guessed that was because I had just come from twenty-degree weather.

I made my way to the baggage claim area and suddenly heard "Mom, Mom!" I looked to where the calls were coming from and saw a group of kids holding beautiful handmade signs and leis to greet me. My kids were great! My two beautiful blonde girls, Sarah and Zoe, and their friends were there to greet me. *How awesome*, I thought. Hugging them, I realized just how much I had missed them.

"Baggage carousel 2," I exclaimed as I headed over, as if I needed to say it—there were only three baggage carousels in the airport, and only one was spitting out bags and suitcases. As we passed the airport coffee shop, I smiled to myself and wondered if my coffee buddy missed me that morning.

I complained incessantly about how miserable the weather had been, and that was the only topic I spoke of. My girls told me how the surf had been so unpredictable and that school sucked.

"Mom, it seems like the storms are coming in every week with hardly a break in the clouds," Sarah said.

"But the temperature has been a consistent seventy-five to eight-five," Zoe added.

"How has school been?" I asked.

"School sucks, and boys are stupid. We missed you, Mom."

"I love to hear that, and I missed you guys as well."

They wanted to hear all about the big city and the adventures their mom had experienced in New York. But of course, they also wanted to tell me more about what they had been up to, and so listening was mostly what I did. That's what moms were for, after all, and I loved being a mom—always had!

Finally, we arrived home. It felt so good to be there. I spent the first two days mostly lying around, recouping from jet lag, and getting unpacked. Then it was back to work. A career of site development was not generally a woman's top career choice, but I always had loved seeing a site change along the way. I also enjoyed seeing the shocked look on a man's face when I was introduced as the project manager.

>-┆-◆>-•-O-•-<◆-┆-<

This day I was flying over to one of the smallest islands in the chain. I was scheduled to oversee a small project as a favor for an old colleague. As the Cessna screeched to a halt, my coffee spilled, and I laughed. I'd never had that problem before being in New York. I still hated the taste of coffee, but I seemed to be taking it when it was offered on every flight now. Ah, these short flights were amazingly enjoyable: you got on, you got your drink, and you got off, that quick. The way a flight should always be!

My phone started ringing as we were taxiing. I pulled my cell phone out of my bag but couldn't make out the number calling me. I was prepared to holler into the receiver, "Hey, I haven't even gotten into my rental car yet!" Then I noticed the call was coming from a New York number. I immediately thought that there must be something wrong at the spa.

"Hello," I answered cautiously.

"Hello, Tia. Did you get home all right?" I recognized the voice, and it took my breath away.

"Yes," I said. I could barely get out the simple word. "Mr. Boss. I mean Mike. Hello. Sorry, I'm just getting off a plane and can't hear very well," I stammered.

"What, you are just getting home now?" he asked.

"Oh, no, I'm back at work and have flown to another island for the day. My day job, you know." I laughed.

"Yeah, so I was just down by the spa, and I saw the manager. She seems to be doing a great job. The business was full, and that girl you hired at the front desk really knows how to sell product."

"Receptionist," I said, interrupting him. "She is called a *reception-ist*." I smiled, happy things were going well.

"When do you think you will be back? I really think you need to be here supporting your team for a while," Mike told me matter-of-factly.

"Well, when does the earth thaw out over there?" I laughed, hoping that would buy me a few seconds to get my thoughts together. I really hadn't expected a call from Mr. Boss himself so soon. Unless something was really going wrong, I guess I'd never expected a call from him at all.

As I disembarked the small plane, I saw the foreman making his way over to me. "Hello, Tia. Here's your keys," he said as he handed me my rental keys.

I caught them but really wasn't paying attention. It seemed I was always distracted when I was talking to Mr. Boss Man. Struggling to focus, I took the phone from my ear for a few seconds.

"Thanks, John. Will I see you this afternoon at the site?" I questioned.

"Who is that you are talking to on the phone?" John asked. He was always very insecure about his job.

"Oh, uh, just the car rental guy." I didn't want to have to go into detail.

Then I heard that familiar demanding voice on my phone. "Who the heck are you talking too?" Mr. Boss asked. I found that I liked his gruff voice.

I quickly said the first thing that came to my mind. "Hey, let me call you back in a minute. I have to get my car."

"Uh … okay, whatever," Mike replied, and then he was gone.

Then it was back to business. I needed to take a hold of myself because I was acting like a teenager, all flushed and telling lies. I walked to the rental car with John while he brought me up-to-date on what was happening and what progress had been made.

As I drove to the site, I quickly called Mike back, and to my relief there was no answer. But within minutes my phone rang back.

"Hello, Mike. I am sorry. I'm having a really busy day. Fridays are always the same for me. Let me call you tomorrow; I will be more relaxed over the weekend. I'm glad there are no problems."

"Huh, okay. I'll talk to you then," Mike replied, almost sounding disappointed.

I hung up and got on with my day.

CHAPTER 3

My Girls

Saturday was always my day with the girls, and every Saturday started the same way: watching a Lifetime movie and during commercial breaks preparing for whatever plans we had for that day.

That Saturday, we were going for a hike at my favorite bay, just a short drive to a remote place on the island where it was all cliffs and lava rock. Not too many tourists went there because there were no sandy beaches, and hikers were few since the trail was short. The trail was mostly used by the surfers for the afternoon swell.

It was a good day for taking photos I could use as screen savers, for which I was famous. I called them my desktop photos. Although I never seemed to get them edited, I had a million and one of them on my phone. I was just like my teenage girls, only with them it was selfies all the time.

I looked ahead to where Sarah and Zoe were playing in the water. I saw the currents pulling. The tide pools were full of action, and the fish darted to and fro. I worried about the girls getting caught in the rip tides. I knew they weren't paying attention because I heard them giggling. I quickly caught up to them and joined in to be Mother Watchful. We loved exploring our world together.

Sarah fell to her waist in the water, and we laughed—until we saw an eel dart by. I started getting a little more nervous. Suddenly, my butt started buzzing. I jumped around only to realize that it was my cell phone. Zoe laughed at my antics and then promptly fell on her butt as well. Now we were all laughing uncontrollably.

After everyone made it safely back to shore, I realized that I should see who had been calling me. Luckily, my phone hadn't gotten wet. The girls charged off on the hike as I reached into my back pocket. I looked at the caller ID and saw that it was Mr. Boss. It was 6:30 p.m. on the East Coast. I hoped there was nothing wrong. I was certain the manager would have called me. *She was a great choice and very responsible. Knows this business very well*, I reminded myself.

"Okay, girls," I called out, "keep hiking. I have to make this call."

He answered quickly.

"Hello," I said.

"Hello. Is that you, Tia?"

"Yes, Mike, I'm just returning your call. Is everything okay?"

"Yes, everything is fine. What are you doing?" he asked.

"I'm just hiking," I told him. I felt a little indignant about his question.

"Who with?"

I smiled because he sounded jealous. "Well, if you really must know, I'm hiking with my girls. Is there something wrong?" I repeated.

"No, no, no. I'm just returning your call."

"What? You are returning my call?" I asked, confused.

"Yes, you called me a few minutes ago. What is going on?" His gruff voice was coming out now.

"Oh my gosh, I must have butt-dialed you. What did you hear?" I asked, a little embarrassed.

"Just a lot of giggling and screaming," he said more calmly.

I told him what had happened and that I would call him the next week for an update on the business. He assured me that all was going well and reinforced that I should be there more to make my presence known. I agreed. After all, he had given me deep discounted rent until the spa showed a profit. *How could I not commit to having another month out there?* I thought before saying good-bye.

His words echoed in my mind after the call ended. *Hmm, I liked that voice. Solid, masculine, and confident.* I sat down on a large rock that seemed placed there just for me and gathered my thoughts. I began to picture him. He was about 5'9" with a stocky build, a kind of natural bulk to his neck, shoulders, and back. I smiled broadly when the image of him became more vivid in my mind. His hind end was rather muscular too. I guessed going to the gym three times a week didn't hurt, but most of it, I could tell, was a natural build, and his fitness came from hard work.

I realized I had been daydreaming awhile when I saw how far the girls were ahead of me. "Hey, girls, wait up," I called out, and then I quickly glanced to see if I had any other calls. But it was just the one from Mike, which would be present in my mind all day that day. I quickened my pace to catch up to my girls. We spent a wonderful day together, and I was fully aware of a strange aura surrounding me. I felt very happy and content.

The next weeks were hectic with the construction company. I tried very hard to keep Mr. Boss out of my mind, and I purposely did not call him. Sunday night rolled around—our sit-down, nice dinner night. On these evenings, we had good conversations and planned what everybody's upcoming week would hold. Nothing was ever boring—hockey competitions, surfing thrills, Mom flying from island to island—but we kept each other on track.

I picked that night to inform the girls of the trip I would need to take and the plan that it would be a month or so long. Their disappointment was inevitable, and I watched their beautiful faces turn sad. I quickly said, "Hey, let's all go—we could make it a vacation." That made them perk up.

They were so tired from their weekend activities that even the excitement of the upcoming trip wouldn't keep them awake that night. For me, though, I knew sleep would be difficult because Mike's voice kept running through my head. It sounded strong and secure, and it made me feel the same way. I lay in bed thinking about him as the full moon shone in through the window and a lovely island breeze drifted over my body. I thought about the conversation at the golf club we'd had while having coffee.

I recalled also our conversation about work, when he had mentioned how he loved doing what he was doing. "I know that I am financially secure and don't need to do physical labor anymore, but I would never ask my guys to do something I wouldn't do. I work six to seven days a week, running my companies and putting out fires, but like I said, it is not rare at all for me to help the guys frame a house or asphalt a road," he had said, smiling as he spoke.

My insecurities swept in, and I wondered whether he was insinuating that I couldn't physically do what the guys do on a job site. Come to think of it, Mr. Boss had not shown any interest in what I did here in Hawaii. I wondered, could it be that he too was a little intimidated by a woman doing what a man would normally do? There was so much to learn. I thought maybe I should shut up and let him ask me about my life the next time we were together.

CHAPTER 4

Getting to Know Mr. Boss

"Mom! Mom, help!" echoed a voice down the hallway. "I can't find my white bathing suit top."

"Oh my goodness. Sarah, why are leaving days always so hard for you? I have had the packing list on your door for a week now," I called back to her.

I called out to my organized one, Zoe, to help find the suit lest we all pay the price the entire way to New York.

"Didn't you just have it on in the hot tub last night?" Zoe asked.

"No, for your information, I wore your white Guess top last night," Sarah shouted defiantly.

"What? Mom, that was already packed!" she wailed. "What else did you take out of my bag? You are so selfish. I am not helping you."

"Girls, c'mon. You will not be living in your bathing suits like you do here. Anyway, one will be plenty. Let's just get these bags to the curb; the car will be here in ten minutes. Zoe, check the flight status, and please make sure the boarding passes are set in my phone. I have a few things to print before I pack up my laptop."

Zoe immediately went to check.

"Stop giving dirty looks, Zoe. Let's just get going," Sarah yelled.

I had learned not to take things too seriously with them. In ten minutes they were always best friends again, and I would still be ticked off, so I was better off just ignoring most of the fights. This newfound attitude came with a lot of aggravation and self-control. But I had come a long way, baby!

"Mom! … Mom! The car is here," Sarah shouted.

"Yes, yes, I hear you!" Geez, it was like I was three. Sometimes I wondered what I ever did before I had teenagers to tell me how to do things. I mean, how did I ever manage? My girls were the sweetest, most considerate kids, but they were teenagers, and when they thought they could get the upper hand, it was like the young lion going in for the kill—the lion that thinks he needs to show all he's got whenever he can, making sure the old lion doesn't forget it too soon. Then when the time is right, he'll go for it.

Why else would they gang up on you over a lipstick color choice, or the width of your belt? Ha. Kids.

"Mom! Helloooo, did you hear me? What are you looking for? We have to go!" Zoe called impatiently.

"I can't find my glasses," I said, searching my bag.

"Your glasses are on your head!" they both called in unison.

They both erupted in laughter at the old lady. I knew they would need me at lunchtime, so I just smiled to myself. Okay, maybe I did have a way of exaggerating a little. My girls had a lot more respect for me and others than most teenagers did these days.

I loved that I had molded my career so that I could take them with me on trips like this. I knew that in a few short years they would both be in college and getting on with life away from me. I made a pact with myself that moment that this trip would be a great bonding one for all of us.

Finally, we arrived at the airport and got checked in. On the plane we all sat together holding hands, as per the norm on takeoff, and waited for that familiar rush of the engine. It pushed us back in our seats, and then we smiled at each other. Up, up, and away went!

For the next eleven hours I would be thinking of all the work that needed doing once we landed. The girls were excited to get off the rock for a while, but I knew that as soon as we landed, they would be busy updating Facebook and texting the friends they had left behind. I wondered whether Mr. Boss remembered what day we were arriving. He had a lot going on and probably wouldn't remember.

The seat belt sign was turned off, and very soon the drink cart came by. The girls asked for a soda, and I decided to have a glass of wine. I thought that might help me doze off before dinner was served, but sleep evaded me; my mind was full of Mr. Boss.

He had a few qualities that mirrored mine. I knew that because not only had I witnessed them myself; I also had heard people around him saying some of the same things that I heard people say about me: "you are loyal almost to a fault," "you are always on the go," "you work too much," "you are a perfectionist," and "you are always giving way too much." Those were great qualities and good thoughts.

The remainder of the flight was uneventful, and soon we were preparing for landing at the JFK International Airport in New York.

>—⊶—○—⊷—<

Upstate New York

I was so incredibly tired. What in the world had I been I thinking? Why did I plan to go to the spa this morning? At least it was warm out.

"Okay, girls, I will be back in a few hours with breakfast. Go ahead and sleep longer," I called out. Some groaning was all I heard.

I stepped out into a beautiful day, with the sun shining in the blue sky. It was vastly different from my memories of the gray sky and cold temperatures. I even heard the birds that morning, and the walk was not even that long. The coffee store was bustling, and I heard a familiar voice coming from behind the counter. I hadn't ever thought that voice would be a good memory.

"Can I get you the usual?"

I thought fond thoughts as I realized my daily visits to the coffee shop had indeed been a good time for me. This time I didn't even have to look up before I answered.

"Yes, black, small, to go." I put my exact change on the counter and a tip in the jar.

"Yes, ma'am. Thank you."

I went on my way, not even drinking half the coffee, but it did feel good in my hands. During the walk I felt like I was in a dream. I felt like I was walking the same walk I had when I was a child. A strange feeling.

The manager was just opening the spa as I walked up. "Hello, Tia. I didn't expect you would be up here this early. How was the trip?"

"Hi, Annie. It went as well as it could, traveling with teenagers," I said with a laugh. "The spa looks and feels wonderful. You are doing a great job."

"Thanks, Tia. I love what we do here. The staff is excellent, and the clients are very happy with the products. We are getting a lot of referrals." Annie beamed proudly.

"Yes, I have heard how well it is doing. I want to do a quick once-over of the business, of course, and then please grab all the files I have requested. I want to get back to the girls."

"Yes, certainly. You should bring the girls in for a treatment," Annie suggested.

"Good idea. They would love it. We need to get our stuff together and then meet an employee of Mr. Boss. He is going to take us to the apartment that we will be staying in. I need to make sure the girls are ready to go, so we don't keep anyone waiting."

Annie gave me a tour through the spa, pointing out a few things that needed my attention while I was there. I was most impressed with everything. I took the files and headed back to the hotel to get the girls.

Walking through the side streets lined with beautiful trees, some with flowers, some just vibrant green, and past driveways lined with purple and yellow flowers, all so bright and full of life, I began to realize this place had its own beauty. The air was so fresh. I took a deep breath. The fresh air in the islands was different and more fragrant at times. But then there were the days when the Big Island volcano was acting up, and vog—volcanic smog—would set heavy on our little paradise, making the air thick and ugly. I wondered whether the air here ever got thick or hard to breathe.

>─┤◆├─○─┤◆├─<

While we waited in the parking lot for our escort, the girls and I got lost in a game of photo tag with our phones—easy to do in unfamiliar surroundings. I didn't even notice the black pickup that pulled up in a parking space a few spaces down. I twirled around with the grace of a baby deer on ice, and I saw Mr. Boss looking out the open window, relaxed and laughing as he watched our game unfold.

Embarrassed, I fought for words to explain why my girls were being silly and blah-blah-blah. He just smiled.

"Would you like to follow me to the apartment?"

"Yes, of course."

I'd had no idea he would be coming himself. He was so busy. I also had no idea why I was so embarrassed. I stumbled to get the keys and get into the car while trying to get the girls to stop laughing.

"Mom, who is that? Mom, why are you so red? Mom ..."

"That's enough," I hissed so he wouldn't hear. "I have to do business with this guy. This is serious, and we need to put on our business faces right now, girls!" They knew when it was time to be serious. I proudly introduced them. Mike gave them his hand and smiled broadly. He appeared happy to meet them. We casually chatted for a few minutes and then climbed into the car to follow him to our summer home.

"Wow, nice place," Sarah stated as we pulled in behind the black pickup.

"Where is the pool?" Zoe questioned. "I'm really hot."

Mr. Boss pulled out a set of keys and opened the door for us to step inside. "You should be comfortable here for the next few months. I see my team has put in some furniture for you," he said, looking around.

"Yes, this is great. I didn't expect this. I also didn't expect for you to show us the apartment. That's nice." I smiled, nervously.

"My pleasure," he said, grinning and looking into my eyes.

I quickly turned away. "Girls, go pick out your rooms. Mike and I need to talk some business."

As they ran to the back of the apartment, Mr. Boss and I walked into the kitchen and started our business talk. We went over a few items and agreed to meet the next morning at one of his restaurants for coffee, to discuss future plans for the business.

After he left, I went to check things out with the girls. The apartment had everything they could've wished for.

"So how do you like it?" I asked them.

"We love it!" they screamed, jumping up and down excitedly.

Mike had really gone overboard for us. We got ourselves unpacked and that afternoon discovered the pool, the gym, and the nearest shopping mall. The girls were ecstatic about the apartment complex, particularly because they had their own Wi-Fi in their rooms.

⊱┈◈┈❍┈◈┈⊰

The next morning I spent a few extra minutes getting ready. When I said good-bye, the girls noticed.

"Wow, Mom! You look beautiful," Zoe commented, giggling.

"Is our mom a little smitten with the big hunk, Mr. Boss?" Sarah laughed.

"Don't be so silly, the two of you. It's ..."

"Right, Mom," said Sarah, cutting me off. "Enjoy your day." They both continued laughing. It made me happy to see their approval.

I arrived at the restaurant before him and immediately ordered—a coffee, of course. It seemed I had become addicted to coffee.

Mr. Boss rushed in shortly after, and I said, "Ten minutes early is on time." We were a lot alike that way too, always rushing somewhere.

He made no excuse. "Coffee?" he shouted at the waitress as he entered. Everybody jumped a little when he came into the room. Why, I couldn't quite figure that out at that point, other than it seemed he paid half the town's paychecks. His coffee arrived before he had time to sit down.

"Tia, you want anything?"

I gestured to my cup. "I'm good." I looked up at the waitress. "I would like to order two breakfast sandwiches to go in about thirty minutes please."

"Will do," she said.

"Well," he said, smiling that infectious smile, "did you three get settled in?"

"Yup, and of course, Sarah and Zoe think they have died and gone to heaven in that apartment."

We both laughed.

We soon got down to business, and Mike offered me an extra office that he happened to have. It was available in his complex just up the road from the shopping center. It came complete with hot coffee, a printer, and a friendly office staff. I accepted graciously because I knew I was in for a long haul, trying to complete the workload back home and make this change-over seamless. *A huge plus that Mr. Boss's office happens to be there too,* I thought.

He interrupted my thoughts. "Friday nights, at my golf course, the staff puts on a great prime rib dinner. If the girls and you would be interested, we would love to see you there," he said sincerely.

"Sure, sounds wonderful. That is, if I can find it," I laughed.

"Here's your sandwiches, Tia," the waitress said, breaking in.

"Oh, thanks. I guess I better get these back to the girls." I said good-bye and rushed out.

As I walked down the sidewalk, I discovered I was a little dizzy. I wondered if I had been giggling too much. I wondered whether the other diners could see that I was speechless. What was it that this man did to me? My phone rang and brought me back to earth.

I pulled out my phone and looked at the screen. Guess who? *Oh my god, does he feel this too?* I thought.

"Tia, it's me."

"Yes?"

"Um, I guess I'll pay for your breakfast sandwiches?"

"Oh my gosh, I am so sorry. I'll come right back," I said apologetically.

"No, no, I'll get it, and don't worry. I'll see you Friday if not sooner. Have a good day."

Oh god, that was embarrassing! Once I saw the humor, I just giggled to myself.

>─┼─◄►─•─○─•─◄►─┼─◄

Friday night came around fast, and the girls were just as anxious as I was to get out and see something other than the spa, although they did love the pampering they received at the spa. The golf course restaurant was packed, and the smells wafting from the kitchen were mouthwatering. I guess it had been a long week of eating frozen meals.

We were seated. We ordered what had been suggested, the house specialty of prime rib. It wasn't long before one of the girls spotted Mr. Boss. He waved and immediately came over to sit down and talk. He showed a very friendly side to the girls and asked them all about their life in Hawaii.

Sarah immediately took over. "What I love about Hawaii is the informal, everyone-pitches-in atmosphere," she began.

Zoe looked ticked that Sarah was stealing the stage.

"Most people just pull up to the beach, bring out the cooler, and grill. They are good to go all day. It's the perfect place, and everyone has something they love to do at the beach. Some of the guys just sit around drinking beer, telling stories, watching the girls. Or they fish," she said, smiling confidently.

"That sounds pretty cool, Sarah," Mr. Boss commented, looking most interested.

Zoe immediately saw her chance to speak up. "Ah, yes," said Zoe, giving a look to Sarah. "Kinda the same thing they would do anywhere else, I guess, but the sweet part is there is no cleanup! The younger crowd surf, boogie-board, snorkel, paddle-board—just about whatever kind of water sport you can think of, they do."

"Do you snorkel or do any of those things?" Mr. Boss asked.

"Of course, I do. I do them all," Zoe boasted.

Then Sarah jumped back in. "The children hang out playing in the sand, and when it starts getting too hot in the afternoon, they venture out into the little tide pools. Generally we get trade winds, so the temperature is perfect. Just about everything about our home is perfect. At the end of the day, everybody loads up their beach goodies and coolers and then heads home," Sarah said proudly.

It was my turn to step in now. "Not quite. It's home to unpack the truck and rinse off the surf boards, and then there is the weekend cleanup to be done, right, girls?" I asked, looking at them for agreement. I knew they hated that part. Somehow I wanted him to know that I did make my girls pull their own weight.

Sarah inquired about the layout of the golf course between bites of her meal, and Mr. Boss explained in detail about his golf course and other developments. It was nice to hear the excitement in his voice as he spoke about certain details. I wouldn't have expected a man of his caliber to even consider the importance of color and style.

I began to realize he was even more like me than I'd thought. He was devoted to his family and not all about business, although it did have an important place in his life. I learned that he was a compassionate man who sat on a board for a large children's charity. He was devoted to his mom and his daughter, who both lived with him. He also had a stepson who lived in Colorado with his wife and two sons. Mike had been separated from his own wife for what sounded like a year or so. Mike sounded excited about being a grandpa! He didn't get to see his stepson as much as he would like to. *Wow*, I thought, *no wonder everybody puts up with him being so gruff with them. He has a soft side too.* The girls were shifting in their seats, bored with this kind of informative talk.

"Mom, can we go walk on the golf course?" Zoe asked.

I glanced over to Mr. Boss as if to ask if he approved. He smiled and nodded his head at them, and off they went.

The lights were soft, and all the other voices had faded; we were alone. All I heard was Mr. Boss speaking, but his voice wasn't bossy anymore. Maybe I had grown accustomed to the voice, and now he was just Mike. I liked his strong jawline and his rugged, masculine face. His eyes were soft brown like mine, and I had never realized before how round they were. I guess I hadn't had time to look at his eyes long enough to study them. He sat with authority, and I was proud to be sitting there with him. Not that I was his date, but I was happy just to have his attention; it made me feel good.

Of course, I saw a few glances in our direction. I knew everyone here knew I was new in town. But I was also sure they knew exactly who Mr. Boss was or wasn't with.

"Don't you think?" he asked me.

I had no clue what he was talking about. I had been daydreaming. "Uh, what? I'm sorry. I was just looking for the girls," I lied.

"I said, I really like your new manager. I think she will do great."

"Oh, yes, I agree," I stammered. Of course, he was talking about work. I found myself disappointed. I saw the girls approaching the table, and I knew our time alone was over.

"Mom, are you ready?" Zoe asked.

"Yes, I am. Can I get the bill please?"

"No, don't worry about it. I got this."

"No, really. You got my breakfast," I joked.

"True, but I got this. I invited you out, remember? Thanks for coming." He smiled, and a glimmer flashed in those honest eyes.

"Thank you."

There was a moment of silence before Sarah broke in. "So Mom, do you think we can bake brownies tonight?"

"You can. I am going to bed. It's up early for me tomorrow. I want you girls to thank Mike for dinner."

They thanked him and headed outside to the car. I stood up and extended my hand to thank him. I was surprised when he took my hand and lightly kissed my cheek. I floated out of the restaurant. When I looked back, he had a big grin on his face and a glimmer in his eyes.

We drove home in silence. My girls were very intuitive, and they knew their mom was starstruck. Once we were inside, I kissed them good night.

"Thanks for a fun night, Mom," Zoe said.

"Sweet dreams, Mom. I like Mike," Sarah said, surprising me. She was not one for volunteering her feelings.

As I lay in bed that night, the crickets were loud, disturbing me as I tried for that early sleep I had been bragging about. Or was it that twinkle in those brown eyes I couldn't get out of my mind?

>─┼─◆>─○─<◆─┼─<

As the weeks went by, all too quickly, we experienced many hot, humid days. The humidity was a little different than in Hawaii, and it took a bit of getting used to. The girls and I discovered shopping in the city. I loved my time with Sarah and Zoe that trip.

Mr. Boss stopped into the spa two or three times a week, but it seemed like I was never there when he stopped in. I found myself making excuses to visit his office more times than necessary, but I almost never saw him. When I did, he was generally in meetings. We only ever shared a quick glance. I knew if I needed anything, his office staff would be at my disposal, but all I really wanted was to sit with him for a moment.

I wanted to look into his soft brown eyes and see that everything was going to be okay. I wanted to see that he saw I could do this. What was wrong with me? I had never needed or wanted a man's approval before. I began to realize what was happening, and the more I tried to resist my feelings, the more those very feelings persisted.

Weeks went by, and before I knew it, we were readying ourselves to head home. It had been a great time, and I had accomplished all I needed to do with my employees. I was not certain that the numbers for the spa were where they needed to be for Mike's lease agreement. I would definitely need to talk with Mr. Boss before leaving.

I called his office to set up a meeting, and to my surprise he was out of town. *Well, my goodness*, I thought, *that's just like a man to up and leave!* Then I calmly reminded myself that I had never told him I was leaving either.

My girls were a little upset that they wouldn't get to say good-bye to Mike. The day before we left, I took them to his office, hoping we would run into him—for the girls' sake, I told myself. Naturally, he wasn't there. The girls wrote him a little note and left it on his desk. His assistant, Clare, assured them that he would get it.

I was able to read the note that Sarah wrote over her shoulder. She told him how nice it had been to meet him and how sorry she was she didn't get to say good-bye. She thanked him for all the help he had given me because she knew how hard her mom worked, and sometimes that was taken for granted. She finished the letter by saying how good it had been to meet someone else in her mom's corner.

As the car sped along the highway, it was a good feeling to be heading back to the islands, ending our time in New York together.

≈ CHAPTER 5 ≈

Back to Our Island

Whenever I traveled, I always tried to get home on a Thursday or Friday night so that I could have a full weekend to recover. This time was no different. We had the full weekend ahead of us, and since I had the girls with me, I wasn't turning on my phone. If there was an emergency, I was confident Annie could handle it. Plus, this gave me total freedom from wishing or hoping for a call from Mr. Boss.

When Monday morning arrived, I turned on my phone to see that I had five voice mails from Mr. Boss. That gave me a certain satisfaction. I smiled confidently to myself before I quickly called him to make sure nothing was wrong.

"Mike, is everything okay? I just got your calls," I said, concerned.

"Why don't you answer your phone on the weekend?" He was almost shouting. He sounded more than a little perturbed.

Good! I thought. "Well, it was a travel weekend, and we were tired and—"

"Why didn't you tell me you were leaving?" he said sternly, cutting me off.

"I tried to, but you were out of town, remember?" I said.

"Didn't you know when you were leaving?" I could almost see his brown eyes squinting with anger.

"Well, yes, of course! I left you messages and stopped by your office numerous times, but I was also busy." That sounded really lame now.

He changed the subject to business very quickly, or maybe it had always been business, and I had just twisted it in my head.

"Well, it would be nice to know exactly how the numbers are going over here," he stated sarcastically.

That ticked me off, but I didn't show it. "Mike, I left a spreadsheet with Clare and an outline of all the intentions for the next few months. I asked her to give it to you and explained if you had questions or updates, she could send them to me. I also let her know when I would be available for a phone call with you this week," I explained calmly.

"Well, keep *me* informed, not my office staff. I want to know what is going on." He seemed a bit calmer.

"It is hard to keep you informed if I can never get a hold of you. What do you propose so this will not happen again?" I asked.

"You can always communicate with me via e-mail to Clare, and I will always call you!"

"Will do. Have a good week," I said tongue in cheek.

"You too. Good-bye."

➤·┼·◆〉·•〈O〉•·〈◆·┼·◄

Wow, that was an odd conversation, I thought. Things were definitely back to business with Mr. Boss. I guessed my daydreams of him were just that, although I couldn't help but think there was definitely a spark there. Maybe at this point in my life, I needed a little spark. All I did was work! Maybe the girls were right, and I should pull my head out of the computer files and look at the guys who were looking at me. According to them, there were plenty.

It would've been nice to be confident, but I'd never felt I had much sex appeal. Part of my problem was I'd never had a close intimate relationship that was safe and comfortable. Then there was the issue of my trust being broken so many times at such a young age, making me more guarded than most people.

Sometimes I thought about what it would feel like to be so close to someone that I could talk about anything. I imagined having a time during the day when all the stress just lifted off, and I could be with that one person with whom I could share my innermost thoughts—no judging, no backtalk, just two people who really knew one another. Maybe that's what pillow talk was. It was sad—I was forty-two years old, and I didn't even know what pillow talk was.

A few days went by, and surprisingly, after our last conversation about communicating, Mr. Boss had begun to call me regularly. The more he spoke to me, the more secure I felt that the business was doing well. We had also begun to talk on a personal level. He had started flirting and making sexual innuendos. I kind of liked it, and the phone calls came during my evening hours, so my pillow talk had begun! I loved the teasing talk, and it felt really safe since we were six thousand miles apart. *Brave, aren't I?* I thought. I had to start somewhere.

I kept thinking about how Mike made me feel when I was with him. When he spoke to me on the phone, he brought me to a level of calm that I hadn't felt in, well, ever. Somehow I just felt better. I knew I had to deal with my daily life, but I found myself wishing I could come home to that voice on a daily basis, and that would make everything better.

"Tia!" a voice shouted. Ugh, once again I was ripped from my daydream. "I thought that little weasel bought twenty-five tons of base course for this road? I didn't know we *gave* it to him." My general manager was yelling halfway across a job site. I was certain everybody else heard him as well.

"He did! I mean we did! I mean, I took care of it yesterday! If you would have read my e-mails instead of jumping on me first thing this morning ..." I paused and thought, *How I would love for Mr. Boss to jump on me first thing in the morning.* I was so going to have to tell him that.

"Tia, did you hear me?" Rick scowled, getting my attention back.

"Yes," I said, scowling right back. "I just don't feel like yelling over machinery today when I have sent all the documents to your office, and you have your phone in your pocket. You can look at the paper-work, and then we can talk. Until you are updated, there is no reason to talk ... right?"

I hated to sound condescending, but I was so darn tired of these guys using me to make themselves look like the big dog on the job site. Six months ago, I guess I would have played the game through, but these days I was seeing myself on a more equal field. I guess I could see what I offered on and maybe off the field.

Later that evening, I got what had become the usual call from Mr. Boss.

"So I have to tell you what happened at work today," I said.

"What's that?" he asked.

I sensed that Mike always got a little excited when I told him what ran through my mind during a workday, especially when it was something sexy. I went on to tell him about the incident with my site manager first thing that morning.

"If I may be so bold, Mr. Boss," I teased, feeling most aggressive, "I actually thought of how I would love for you to jump on me first thing in the morning." I couldn't believe what had just come out of my mouth.

"Hmm, that would be great," he said, almost in a whisper. He sounded like he'd been caught totally off-guard.

What did I just say? Who is this person being so provocative with a man she hardly knows? Now you have started something, I thought.

"Tell me what else you thought about," he said, taunting me, a little more enlivened.

"Uh," I stammered. "I thought it's time for me to come and see you. I need you," I said, feeling very stimulated. He must have heard that in my voice.

"How red are you right now?"

"Pretty red," I said.

"You're funny. When can you come back? I miss your red face among other parts of your body," Mike said softly.

"Uh, okay, not sure. I miss you too." I reached up and felt how hot my face was. "I've got to go. My girls are home. I'll call you soon."

"Okay. Call me tomorrow, please? I need you here in a few days. Be ready. It is time!" he exclaimed.

This was it. He must really want me. Good! Now he was doing something about it. Yes! I wanted to do a backflip right at that moment, but I kept it together.

"I will, time difference and all," I said, like I was ordering a sandwich. "Tomorrow I'm on another island all day, so it may be late." My heart was fluttering.

I really liked everything about this guy, this guy who was saying, "Please call me!" I felt the excitement building inside of me. It was time.

Shoot, a few days. Best do as Mr. Boss says, I thought upon hanging up the phone. Suddenly, I realized my body was tingling in places it shouldn't be in the middle of the day. I put my hand to my cheek again. Yes, I could tell it was red.

CHAPTER 6

First Time—Last Time?

"Call me when you are on your way to the airport. I want to know what your exact flight plans are. I know you'll have the girls with you, so call me after they drop you off." Mike sounded anxious.

"I will. Don't worry. Bye," I said reassuringly. The girls and I climbed into the car and headed for the airport. On the way, I gave the usual instructions to my girls that I was sure they knew by heart.

We arrived at the airport, and I kissed and hugged my girls. They smiled at me, having been quite accepting of my trip. I was happy that they were not asking me questions. I waved good-bye as they drove away. I checked in at the curb, went through security, and made my way to the gate before I called Mike. *I am actually doing this*, I thought. I was full of nerves and really excited. I quickly took out my phone and called Mr. Boss.

"Hello? Is that you, Tia? Hey, where are you?"

"I'm at Maui Airport, waiting for the flight departure."

"Thank god. I was nervous that you might change your mind."

"No, no. I want this. Um, so from here, I'm in Sacramento tonight and Chicago tomorrow morning. Tomorrow night, 10:00 p.m. your time, I will be there," I said while searching for my boarding passes.

"Great. I can't wait to see you, Tia."

"Yeah, me too," I said, smiling. I knew he couldn't see me, but he felt me all right. There was this certain connection between us. I was sick with nerves, though, questioning my ability to please him. I knew he had to be very experienced. Not marrying until he was forty had given him plenty of time to sow his oats.

"Call me when you get to California? I hate you being this far away from me," he crooned.

"Mike, it will be after midnight your time. Is that okay?" I was hesitant.

"Yes, of course, call me any hour. I can't get you here quick enough," he said anxiously.

"Me too. Bye."

>─┼─◆─○─◆─┼─◄

I turned on my phone as soon as we hit the tarmac in California, as I always did, to make sure the girls were okay. I knew they would be fine—heck, they were almost eighteen, and I had many friends watching out for them when I was gone—but I still worried. I would always worry. I was a mom after all.

I looked at my phone to see I had three voice mails from Mr. Boss. I smiled and felt most confident about his intentions. I couldn't call him now, though. It was way too late. Although he had told me to call anytime, I decided to wait and postpone the call a little longer.

He rarely left messages, and I hated that. He didn't have voice mail and didn't think other people listened to theirs. At first I'd thought that was strange, but when I witnessed how many calls he would receive in a day, I realized it would be just another thing for him to juggle. I did, in fact, know many people without e-mail, and Mr. Boss was one of them. If I had a reliable assistant, I probably would have let the assistant take care of my e-mail as well.

My next flight was called, and I quickly boarded. Off we went! The rush pushing me back in my seat made my heart flutter even more than usual. I knew that when the plane touched down this time, I would actually call Mr. Boss and hear his voice. Hmm, that voice. I closed my eyes, hoping I could sleep. I knew that I would be sleeping well the next night, in his arms!

What if he discovers my inexperience and fear? As I began thinking, the memories of my childhood abuse flooded my mind. And it had been so long since I'd had sex. I shuddered at the memory of those times I had been called upon to do my wifely duty. This was the first time I had truly wanted a man, and I wanted it to be great. *Oh my god! I am so inexperienced*, I thought. I was hoping he wouldn't be able to tell.

Wait, I thought, *is that what's really going to happen?* Now I was unsure. We hadn't really specified. I guessed, and I hoped, but I didn't know. Suddenly, I went into panic mode. Were we dating? Was this dating in this century? I didn't know. I didn't care. I was almost there. *I sound like a poet*, I thought. As I cracked myself up, I realized I was getting loopy. I must have been getting tired!

>─┤◆⟩─○─⟨◆├─<

"Welcome to Albany."

I had made it to New York. My first instinct was to call Mr. Boss to let him know I had arrived. But I hesitated. I needed to unpack and shower before I saw him. On the other hand, I did want to hear his voice. I made up my mind to place the call, and he answered.

"Hey, hey, guess who's here," I heard myself say.

"What? No way! I thought you weren't in until tonight?" He sounded excited.

"I know," I said, sounding surprised myself. "I was able to catch an earlier flight out of O'Hare. Anyway, I need to get my bags and unpack. I'm dead tired, and of course, I need a shower badly." I waited for his reaction.

"Okay, so give me a call when I can come up."

"Sounds good," I said, a little relieved. Eighteen hours of travel with little to no sleep left a lady a little messy, to say the least. Thank goodness for baby wipes and travel toiletries during the delays. It wasn't a shower, but it was better than nothing.

While waiting for my luggage to hit the baggage claim area, I took the opportunity to brush my hair and put on a little lip gloss. Then it was off to the rental car. I was thankful I had decided to fly directly to Albany instead of NYC this trip. It was much less stressful. At least I got out of the airport area without Rosie "recalculating."

I made it to the hotel drive and could take a breath. Now I just needed to check in to my room and get in that shower and get my hair done before Mr. Boss started wondering why I hadn't called. It had been too many years since a man had come before business. This would've surprised anyone I knew, including my daughters! Maybe not Mr. Boss—he was pretty sure of himself.

Surprisingly, it did not feel that cold outside, maybe because I was nervous and trying to drag my oversized bags out of an undersized trunk! I heard a familiar giggle, and turning around, I saw a black pickup with the window down.

"Do you always just watch people until they notice you?" I said, startled.

"No, just you," he said, smiling warmly.

How could anyone ever be mad at that smile? I thought.

He climbed out and walked over, gesturing toward the bag. "I'll get that."

"Thanks," I said. At first I wanted to hug him, but the moment passed. I realized I must look awful and suddenly felt embarrassed. "Um, I haven't had time to shower yet," I said timidly. I realized that he must have been anxious to see me.

"I can see that," he replied.

"Thanks a lot!"

"I already checked you in—suite 126, this way." He began walking to the end entrance of the hotel. "Where do you want this five-hundred-pound bag?" He smiled as he opened the door to the room.

I walked past him to find the suitcase stand. "Here is good," I said as I propped the stand open next to the wall.

It seemed we were both feeling a little awkward. Somehow we made it to the couch to sit down. We made small talk, which it seemed neither one of us was very good at. We each received a few phone calls that we had to take, but we made them short.

"Well, I should get back to work," he blurted out.

Oh no, you don't. Come by before I can get a shower and then just leave? I waited too long, I thought. Not even realizing what I was doing, I slid toward his end of the couch and awkwardly hugged him.

"Mike, no! I just got here and haven't even gotten to talk to you."

I let go and slid back over to my side of the couch. I watched him while he just stared out the window. I didn't know if he was trying to think of words to say, how to leave, or what. Suddenly, he looked over at me and stood up; in an instant, I was in his arms, being kissed passionately. He gently laid me down on the couch and knelt beside me, still kissing me deeply.

Holy shit, this man could kiss. He stopped. My brain started off on a panic. Why had he stopped? Oh my god. I hadn't brushed my teeth! Crap! I hadn't showered! I sucked at kissing! What could it be?

Then he looked deep into my eyes and asked, "Well?"

"Well?" I questioned back.

"Meet back here in an hour?"

"Oh my god. Oh my god. Yes! In an hour," I gushed.

Before I knew it, the door was closing behind him, and I was in the shower. The warm water caressed my body as I imagined his hands would be doing very, very soon. I suddenly remembered that I needed to shave. I really hadn't thought about it, but I needed to shave *everywhere!*

Forty-five minutes later, there was a knock on the door. *Are you kidding me?* I thought. *Do you not know when a woman says an hour, that means at least an hour and a half? Crap! My hair is not even dry, and I am in a towel.* My mind was chattering away again.

Maybe this was how he wanted me, or maybe he was expecting lingerie. I didn't even own a nightgown, so he was going to get a towel. *Lip gloss, lip gloss,* I thought. *Where is my lip gloss?*

"Knock, knock!"

"Coming," I called out.

"Hey," I said, trying to sound cool. "It's only been forty-five minutes," I said shyly.

"Do you want me to come back?" he asked.

"You're funny, very funny. What you see is what you get," I teased.

I had barely closed the door before he headed toward the bedroom. If I'd had any doubt about what we were doing, I didn't any longer. I made a quick stop in the bathroom to take a few breaths. Apparently, that was all the time he needed to undress.

"I have been thinking about this for a while," he said with a smile when I entered the room, peeking over the covers.

"Can I turn down the lights? I feel nervous. It's been a while for me."

"Whatever you feel comfortable with, Tia."

I turned off the lights but left the door ajar for a little light to stream in.

Ugh, no pressure, Tia. Here goes, I thought. I closed my eyes and let my towel drop to the floor. He reached over, pulling me onto the bed. I started to resist. Hoping he would go slow and gentle, I ordered myself to stop thinking.

"Oh, baby," he moaned.

Okay, so maybe I was doing something right. I kept doing it. Why couldn't I relax and enjoy this like I'd enjoyed that kiss earlier? I felt like I was on stage. I was tense and emotionless, kissing him all over because he apparently liked it.

"Kiss me. Oh, kiss me everywhere," he said.

I am, I am! I thought. Then it hit me: he wanted me to kiss him *there. Not happening!* I thought. I came back up to his face and kissed his mouth. He looked at me, puzzled and a little disappointed. Then without warning, in one motion, he slid his arm around the small of my back and guided me underneath his masculine form.

I was wet with desire from this one move. He gently guided himself into me. I could see in his eyes the pride he felt in giving pleasure to me. I could also tell he sensed my fear.

"I got you, baby," he said gently.

Meanwhile, I couldn't shut my brain off, as per the norm. *God, where did this guy come from?* He was so passionate, tender, and well, I guess just what I needed.

"I've got you, baby. Let go. I've got you."

I closed my eyes and started to move with him. I tried to surrender to nature's ultimate gift, but I couldn't.

"Well," he said gently, "you have some hang-ups, huh?"

"Oh my goodness," I said, breathless. "I am so sorry. It was awful for you, wasn't it?"

"Well, let's put it this way: I have had better. But why wouldn't you go down on me?" he asked.

"Well, I guess … well, I mean … I never … um, I just …"

"What, you mean you never have?" He sounded shocked.

"No," I said, wondering what I was feeling. Was it shame, shyness, a sense of being closed off?

"Really?" he said in disbelief.

"Why is that so surprising?" I asked.

He just looked at me. "What else haven't you done?" he questioned.

I took offense. "What is that supposed to mean?"

"Well, let's see. If you haven't given ... have you received?"

I pulled the covers toward my face and felt the room getting smaller.

"Did I say something wrong?" he continued.

Was he really still talking about this? Couldn't he see this was incredibly uncomfortable for me? Why were we discussing this? People didn't talk about these things!

"Well," he said, continuing to push, "I'm not going away."

"I just never have ... okay?" I blurted out, thinking that would satisfy his rude curiosity.

"You mean to tell me that you have *never* had oral sex?" He rolled over, looking into my eyes.

"No!"

"What about orgasms? You have had those, right?"

"Not really. Can we stop talking about this?" I asked, wanting to crawl into a hole.

"Why?" He sounded astounded. "You can't tell me your ex-husband never asked you to have oral sex."

"I tried once. It's complicated ..." I trailed off as I searched for the words. How was I supposed to explain abuse and pain and all that baggage to someone I just slept with for the first time? All those emotions I had pushed down for years— I didn't want to talk about them. This was one of the very reasons I didn't want people getting close. When I kept people at a distance, I didn't have to explain or remember or feel. Why was he pushing me with this?

"What's complicated about that? Did he never ask again? I find that hard to believe," he said as he lay back on the pillow.

"No, if you must know, I was abused as a little girl, and that is something that I can't do now. I get flashbacks." I had finally gotten it out. The silence seemed to last forever as I fought to hold back the tears over those dreadful memories.

"Tia, I'm sorry. I shouldn't have pushed. I'm such an idiot. I know that must have been very hard on you." I could hear the compassion in his voice. "Who was it?"

"My dad and my grandpa," I said with my eyes lowered in shame.

"I would never hurt you in that way."

As usual someone's phone broke the silence. It was Mike's phone this time.

He answered and listened for a moment. "Yeah," he said, "I'll be right there." He jumped out of bed and immediately got dressed without saying a word, like I wasn't in the room. "I have to go. I'll call you later." In a flash, he was gone.

He hated it! I thought. Sobbing, I pulled the covers over me.

Later ended up being the next day. But that was okay with me. I needed time to process the whole idea of opening up to someone—someone I hardly knew, but then again, I guessed I hardly knew anyone. If people don't get close to you, they can't hurt you. It wasn't that I'd ever really thought about it like that. I just lived my life that way.

Whether or not you realize it, or want to admit what happened, the past is the past, and the truth is the truth. I remembered reading those words in a book when I was in therapy. I kept wondering how to explain the experience of child abuse from the inside. I wanted to try to explain what my world had been like when I was sexually abused. People had to remember that this was the thinking of a child.

I knew that this subject must be addressed with Mr. Boss. I would try to remember those words when the time came.

CHAPTER 7

Learning about Each Other

W̶hen Valentine's Day weekend rolled around, and I had no call from Mr. Boss, I was ticked. Really, sometimes I thought that I was just a piece of bad ass that he had tried out. I didn't blame him in a way.

Women were always waiting around for men. Well, I would be darned if I was waiting around in this freaking frigid air, watching all the loving couples come to the spa for their romantic getaways. I deserved to sulk. I had struggled all month to put this romantic marketing campaign together. I'd been listening to all the stories of my employees' Valentine's plans. I was not waiting around just in case something happened, and he decided I was important. Sometimes my strong self-assured twin would show up, and when she did, I became a woman who put herself first and who was capable of moving above all the romantic mystery, or should I say the lies we feed ourselves.

Oh, how I would have loved for Mr. Boss to show up with a single flower of any kind and say these words: "I'm glad you understand how busy I am, but later tonight I will whisk you away and show you a great time!"

A girl could dream. But it sure looked like he wouldn't be whisking me away that night. I wondered why men seemed to be lacking that gene, the one that would alert them to a woman's emotional needs. If they had it, they would know that it was an emotional, crushing blow to a woman when a man told her he would call and then didn't.

It seemed to me this was one of those nights I could drive myself crazy thinking, or maybe obsessing, about where he was. It was easy to get out of hand with it—was he with another woman or whooping it up with the boys? Maybe he was just working late and lost track of time. We women could drive ourselves crazy imagining all sorts of silly things. It really didn't matter. The men in our lives showed up sooner or later with a great excuse (though we know there is no logical excuse; communication capabilities are everywhere, so if they really wanted to get in touch, they would), and we choose to believe it, but we always hold the moment in the back of our minds.

For Valentine's Day, I decided to pack my bag for the city and go to the dog show. We certainly didn't have any opportunities like that in Hawaii, so I decided I would take advantage of a free weekend! The spa was under control, and I had worked too hard to sit around and mope through another weekend. My girls would be proud if only they knew. I wished I could tell them this learning lesson.

What if at the last minute Mr. Boss decided to stop by or call perhaps? *Hmm, let's see,* I thought. *Every one of his office staff has been bragging all week of their weekend plans. You told them you're going to the NYC dog show, even though you planned on canceling at the last minute if he showed up. If he really wants to, he'll be able to find you.*

The train ride into the city was unbelievably cold but nevertheless beautiful. I watched the kids playing on the frozen Hudson River. As I made my way to the café car to get some hot coffee, more to warm my hands than to drink, a light snow started outside the windows. It was so beautiful that it made me forget how cold I was for a moment. Amazing! I took a ton of photos and texted them to my girls. Very soon, my cell phone rang.

"Hello, my treasures," I said, knowing they would have me on speakerphone.

"Mom, we just got your text and pictures! We are so jealous. We want to come to the dog show with you," Sarah said, faking a whine.

"We have to watch it on TV ... but Mom, we will look for you in the crowd!" Zoe squealed.

"I'm only going to the small dog segment, and the rest of the time I will be shopping." I quickly realized that I should not have mentioned shopping.

"That's great, Mom. Buy us something? Please, please ..."

"Hey, I have to go. Talk to you later." I hung up. The train was about to arrive in the city, and that made me feel better about the heartache I was suffering.

"Ms. Malone, we didn't expect you so early. Can you wait for your room?" the desk clerk asked me.

"Yes, sure. How long will it be?"

"Well, maybe just an hour or so."

"Okay, that's fine. I will head up to Macy's for a while."

I handed my bags over graciously to the clerk and then gritted my teeth as I headed out into the bitter cold once again. Ugh! Four blocks to Macy's in this wicked February weather. How New Yorkers did this, I would never know. There was definitely not enough coffee in the world to entice me to live here in this bitter cold. *May as well shop*, I decided, *and shop, I shall!* One thing I had learned to do on my trips to New York was shop.

Hours later, as I left the bright lights of retail and headed into the dim lights of the city streets, I realized that I had forgotten how early it got dark in New York. *Oh geez! It's okay*, I told myself. *It's only four blocks.* I quickened my pace and made it back in record time, frozen but well.

"Oh ... oh no, Ms. Malone," the desk clerk stuttered. "I am so sorry. I gave your room to an elderly couple. When you didn't come back, I thought we could have another one cleaned in time. I apologize. Would you mind waiting in the lounge just a few more minutes?"

Seriously? I mean, I was accommodating, but this was a little ridiculous. I didn't have to utter a word. The disappointment must have been written all over my face.

"Uh, um" the clerk stammered, "please let us pay for your dinner. That is the least we can do for this inconvenience." He was most embarrassed. I could see his face getting redder by the second.

"That's fine. I'm really not hungry. I just want a hot shower because I'm frozen!"

"I understand." He quickly turned back to his computer and smiled. "I can upgrade your room. I will give you a suite for the night. Please forgive my misjudgment. Will that be okay with you, Ms. Malone?" he asked.

"Yes, thank you," I said, smiling. "That will be nice. Thank you very much, and you are forgiven!"

"Great. Then I will set that up. The view is outstanding. It is a corner suite with a view of the Empire State Building, which has been illuminated for Valentine's Day, and ..." He went on and on, and I could see he was very proud of himself.

How nice, I thought as I signed the paperwork. I just wanted to get into the friggin' hot tub.

As I followed the bellhop, I was dreaming of a nice Jacuzzi tub with some champagne. It was Valentine's Day, and he did say a suite. Ah yes, this might not be bad after all.

I wondered what Mr. Boss was doing. Probably trying to make it with his estranged wife. A man worth that much money wouldn't let it walk away with the wife. Who was I trying to kid? And here I was in NYC by myself, freezing with a great view of the Empire State Building all illuminated in red for this great holiday. I didn't know whether to laugh or cry.

"Ms. Malone ..."

I was jolted back to reality. "Yes?"

"Will you be dining with us this evening?" he asked, holding open my room door.

"No, no thank you."

"Yes, of course. Tomorrow night is reservations only. Please make certain you call the desk before 10:00 a.m."

"I'm only staying for tonight."

I handed him a generous tip when he put the bags down. The door had closed behind me before I could take in the room and whip around to let him know there had been a mistake. This was not the suite I had been promised. I wasn't spoiled by any stretch of the imagination, but this was utterly ridiculous. The room was barely the size of a broom closet.

Oh well, things just got better and better. What else could go wrong? I got my bathroom bag out and headed to the bathroom for that hot tub. Nope, not even a small tub. I could barely even fit in the shower.

There were the corner windows that reached from floor to ceiling as promised. And as I opened the curtains, I saw the most spectacular view. Yes, it was the Empire State Building illuminated in red, with a huge red heart positioned on the side.

"Beautiful … just beautiful!" I said out loud as the tears rolled down my face. I wished I was sharing this with Mike. *Mike. Oh, Mike, I think I love you.*

I took a tiny man's shower, cranked the heater up, and left the window curtains open all night. Good night, Empire State Building! I fell asleep texting my girls lots of photos of the view, which they could hardly see, but I promised them that it was beautiful.

➤┄◆┄○┄◆┄◄

My phone ringing woke me up. *What the heck?* I thought when I saw the clock. *It's 7:00 a.m.!* The spa wasn't even open yet. I sleepily grabbed my phone as I saw the Empire State Building outside my window. I smiled, remembering my awe at the sight.

"Hello," I said dizzily.

"Tia, where are you?"

"Mike? I am in the city. Why?"

"I have been trying to reach you. The alarms have been going off, and I don't know the codes for the system."

"It is 1-0-2-2," I said, not really comprehending what was happening.

"Okay!" he growled. "I will call you right back."

I lay back on the pillow, trying to make sense of the call. He called back within minutes with a barrage of questions.

"What are you doing in the city? When are you getting back? Who are you with?" All odd questions, and of course, I was not quite awake, but I tried to answer.

"Um, I couldn't reach you, and everyone else was busy for the weekend. I just wanted to get away. I came down to see the dog show and do a little shopping for the girls before I head back home. I am coming back this evening. You didn't return any of my calls. Was I that bad?" I asked, feeling insecure.

"Oh … umm. What? No!" he said. "We had a freeze up in an apartment complex yesterday afternoon. Then a sewer main broke. It's been a hell of a mess here," he explained without missing a beat. There was no "how are you," or "I miss you," or perhaps "Happy Valentine's Day."

"Oh, I see … well, I'll see you when I get back."

"Yes, I'll see you then. Have fun at the show," he said and was gone.

I hung up and realized that if the alarms had gone off, the alarm company would've called my manager. If they couldn't get a hold of her, they would have called the building manager. Something didn't seem right. I called Annie. No one had called her, but she said she would check on whether the alarm had been reset when she got in, and she would let me know. I hung up. I began to question whether Mr. Boss had wondered where I was for Valentine's Day and just didn't know how to ask. Were we more alike than I even thought? Could I dare hope that this guy was into me too?

The dog show was great. I met so many little dog friends, and of course, shopping was always nice, but I had to get back to reality, work, and Mr. Boss. What was I going to do about this hole he kept putting in my heart? Would he keep patching it back up with his little ways, not even realizing what he was doing? Whose fault was that? I questioned myself. I had an entire train ride to figure it out. Back out into the frigid cold once again.

>—I—<>—•—O—•—<>—I—<

At least my hotel back in Albany had a huge tub so that I would be able to warm my bones when I got back. I had also become quite thankful for the warm cookies and coffee they put out in midafternoon. That coupled with not wanting to get out for a jog every morning in the frigid air was putting a few pounds on my rear!

I swung open my room door and realized the maids must have turned down my heat again. Their idea of warm was not my idea of warm! That was definitely one difference Mike and I had. I always had to have my toes in the sheets at least. I smiled to myself. No matter how much he broke my heart, there was always room for a smile. I loved the small memories we had begun to create. I plopped my bag down and headed straight to the heat register, but before I got there, I heard a knocking at the door. When I opened the door, I expected to see the maid, so I blurted out that I didn't need service just as I opened it.

But it was not the maid. "Huh! Oh, hi, Mike!" I managed to get out.

"Hello, yourself. Happy to see you made it back. Weren't you going to call me?" he said, pushing past me.

"Well, I ... uh ... just got here, and who are you to talk about calling?" I quipped.

"I thought you were coming back this morning."

"No, I went to the dog show this morning and caught the train this afternoon. I ..."

"Oh, how was the show?" he said, cutting me off and already half undressed.

I turned away from him, feeling a little mad, but as his arms wrapped around my waist, and I felt his warm breath on my cold neck, I relaxed.

"Did you miss me?" he whispered. I melted once again.

"I ... uh, Mike, I need to turn on the heat," I said hesitantly. *Does he think he can just come in here and take me?*

"Heat!" He smiled. "You and your heat. It's already hot in here, and if it isn't now, I'll make it hot for you!"

"No. I'm seriously cold. Let me turn it up a little. My feet are freezing," I insisted.

"Okay, but then you get your little butt undressed and in this bed pronto. We are about to try a few new things."

"Yes, Mr. Bossy Boss," I teased as I adjusted the thermostat. I hated myself for giving in so easily. I wanted him just as badly, and with him I was up for new things.

"C'mon, c'mon," he growled as I undressed and climbed into the bed beside him. "I have been waiting for you."

I laid my body on top of his, and he slid me down to his waist. I hesitated, a little fearful.

"Stop bossing me. I am not an employee," I whispered. Then I saw that smile—I loved that smile! I felt him harden with just one touch. Intuitively, I kissed the inside of his thighs at the same time I placed my hand on myself. I liked getting to know his body and how quickly it responded to my touch. I liked the control I had, and I liked the pleasure I could give to him.

"Good, baby. That is good. I want you to have a climax, or let me come down on you," he suggested.

"No, this is good like this," I managed to say as I pleasured myself. I could feel something happening, and I was losing control, but I didn't want to regain it. My mouth now enveloped his manhood. It felt unbelievable, and within seconds I climaxed. The throbbing seemed to go on forever.

"Mike, I did it. You did it. We did it," I said, almost proud.

"Oh, my sweet, you were wonderful ..."

Your turn, I thought. I quickly put my lips back on the tip of him. I felt pretty confident I could take it all.

We had a torrid session full of sexual pleasure. When he couldn't stand it any longer, he begged me to come up to him. I sensually slid up beside him. He gently slid on top of me and entered me, sending me into another instant climax. He waited for my panting to settle before he began again. This time I lasted longer as he moved deeply in and out of me.

"My god," he groaned as he stood up. "My legs are hardly working."

"Mine too," I laughed. "Seems like we have this effect on each other."

He lay back down, and we laughed. For me it was a release of long-held emotions.

After we showered and got dressed, we sat down and talked a lot about the plans for the spa. Out of the blue he changed the subject. "What about our plans?" he asked.

"You mean personally or with the lease?" I said innocently.

"Us!" he said and kissed me.

My heart began beating so fast. This was it! He finally wanted to know about us. "What do you have in mind?" I said with a smile, pretending it was more sex.

"I think that we should look for an apartment for you, for us, for the girls. I don't know. All I know is that I want to spend more time with you!" He pulled me close to him.

"That would be great, Mike. I would like that, not to mention how thrilled the girls would be." I jumped up and began dancing around. "Let's find a place that has a gym. I can work out in the warmth before going to the spa to work," I said enthusiastically.

"I'll be keeping you warm. Let's not be worrying about that too much," he said.

I wanted to say something smart like "what about when I can't find you or when you don't answer your phone?" But of course I didn't. We talked a while longer, and then it was time for him to leave.

"I'll call you tomorrow." He kissed my cheek, and after he left, I ran to the window to watch him drive away. Yes! I loved this man.

The next day, I saw Mike arriving at the spa bright and early. His truck pulled up right beside my car. I felt that rush of excitement in my stomach as he got out. Nobody was due here yet. *Maybe we could have a moment in the back*. I turned red just thinking about it.

"Good morning, Tia," he said.

"Morning. You are down here early. Aren't you supposed to be in your office?" I asked as I pushed those naughty thoughts out of my head.

"Well, yes, but I thought I would catch you before you got busy with your day. You are hard to get in the afternoon, and I thought we could plan some time together."

"Really? I wasn't hard to get yesterday afternoon." I smiled.

"You even turn red when you're the one making the sexual comment," he said, grinning.

"I know, I know," I giggled. "Anyway, what's up?"

"Well, I was thinking that we really haven't even shared a proper meal together, so are you up for that tonight?"

"Sure," I said, trying to hide my delight. "Sounds good. What time?"

"You know me and time. I'll call you." Mike didn't like to commit to specific times.

"Okay. Talk to you later then."

He turned to leave, and I smiled, trying not to look disappointed.

I hurried through my day and made all preparations so that the evening shift would not have any issues at all. If they did, they were instructed to call the night manager. I rushed out to buy a new dress for my date, but I couldn't find anything appropriate. It didn't help that I was between sizes.

My phone rang. It was Mike. I hoped he was not on his way already. I'd thought I would have at least another half hour to shop.

"Hey," I said.

"Hey, where are you?" he asked.

"Oh, just shopping."

"I wanted to let you know that I'm running a little late."

What's new? I thought, but at least he was calling. "That's okay. Me too," I said, trying not to sound disappointed.

It really is all right, I told myself. Now I had a little extra time to go to another store. I trudged on to find that special outfit. But I still didn't find it. I decided I better get back to my hotel room and get ready.

>–⊷–◦–⊶–<

Three hours later, I felt like that sixteen-year-old girl once again stood up. Waiting, waiting, waiting! How long was I going to do this? How many times could I let him break this heart? No more. Not one more time! I was writing a letter and leaving it at the front desk. I was leaving tomorrow morning and never seeing him again. It was the only way. I couldn't continue on like this. I sat down and began writing.

> *Dear Mike,*
>
> *I guess I really must say thank you for making me see truly what I deserve. It's not waiting for a man to call me at a hotel room anymore. I must have fallen in love with you somewhere along the way. I didn't want to even admit it to myself, let alone tell you. I have grown with you, and in spite of you, which is a beautiful thing. I don't think you are ready for me, though. You need to at least pick up the phone more than occasionally and*

*let me know what goes on in your head. Maybe I am
to blame for that. I have learned how to express myself
sexually, and now verbally it seems. But I think it's too
late for that. I guess for my next relationship, I will have
learned a few things. Sad, really. I care for you deeply. I
hope our paths cross again. Please don't try to talk me
out of leaving this relationship. Is that what we had?*

Tia

It was a long walk to that front desk. The clerk looked up.

"Hi!" I said. I tried to sound businesslike as I made my request. "I will be checking out in the morning. I need to leave this envelope for a man named Mike. He will pick it up tomorrow sometime. Please be sure he gets it," I said as I pushed the letter across the desk.

"Yes, sure thing," the desk clerk assured me.

Then it was off to bed. That was it. It was all over. The girls would be happy when I arrived home early. I would make an excuse to Annie as to why I had to leave early, but she would be fine. The business had been going fairly well.

My phone ringing woke me up even before my alarm.

"Hello, Mike," I said, trying to sound nonchalant.

"Sorry. I'm so sorry. We had a break-in, and I was with the police till late."

I cut him off before he could say more. "That's fine. I am leaving today anyway. There is an envelope at the front desk for you. I'll talk to you soon." I hung up before he could question me because really, what was I going to say? I just hoped he would get the letter and then leave it alone.

Time to get ready for my long day of travel. I turned on the shower and let it run while I made a cup of coffee and made sure I had packed up all my clothing. A knock at the door interrupted the shower idea.

I exited the bathroom and opened the door. "Mike!" I said in utter shock. It had taken him all of ten minutes.

"Why are you leaving?" he said, pushing his way past me. "And what is at the front desk? A Dear John letter?"

Now I felt stupid. I didn't know why, but I did. "No, just an explanation as to why I am leaving. Do you mind? I was about to take a shower," I told him coldly.

"No, I want to talk to you." He was angry.

"Well, when I want to talk, you have things to do," I said, surprising myself.

"Okay, take your shower." He backed down and softened his tone immediately.

"Thank you. I'll be right out."

"Do you mind if I make a few calls?"

"No, knock yourself out."

I heard his gruff voice on the phone as I stepped into the shower. I was praying that he wouldn't go down to get that letter. I stepped out refreshed and ready to face the conversation. I was relieved to still hear his voice. Maybe that meant he hadn't thought about getting the letter, or he didn't want to know what it said.

I saw him sitting by the window, gazing out with the same look on his face he'd had that very first day we gave ourselves to each other. He was deep in thought. I looked at those dark brown eyes, the same ones I would see in the mirror looking back at me once in a while, the ones that said, "What now, Tia?" I sat across from him. He turned his face to mine and didn't have to say a word. We just looked at each other, our eyes locked. He looked as sad and confused as I felt.

"So?" he said softly.

"So?" I matched his tone.

"Tia, what did the letter say?"

"I don't even remember. Sometimes I feel like an emotional wreck with you, and I felt the only thing I could do is leave. Maybe it's running. I'm not sure if I'm ready to trust yet. I wrote the letter because you don't treat me like I am important to you. I felt a lot of emotions, and some probably weren't even about you. I have a lot going on, and I needed to get it all out. Now I feel better and regret writing it," I said truthfully.

It felt good to see him holding me in his gaze. Even though this might be the end for us, I felt comforted.

"Mike, sometimes I can explain things better if I give an example.

I am not the greatest communicator. I think you know that already, don't you?"

"Know what, Tia? What in heaven's name are you talking about?" He frowned.

"Know how when you don't call, it hurts!" I said right back. "Know that when you say you're going to do something and you don't, it hurts!" I almost sobbed.

"Tia, I am busy. You know that. I have told you business comes first. We had that conversation, and you said you felt the same way. You said that's how it has to be. I thought you of all people understood that."

"Mike, I do understand. But business coming first is different than being respectful of feelings, and there has to be a balance," I said, standing my ground.

I saw the confused look on his face and knew that this was like talking to an eight-year-old kid about biochemistry.

"Just because you have a job to finish or a bid to get in, and it is going to take you all night, that doesn't mean you can't pick up the phone and let someone know or plan ahead," I said, firmly but softly. "Thinking I understand doesn't give you a free pass to break plans every time and not call to let me know what is going on. That is common courtesy to anyone, but to someone you care about, it is a need that must be fulfilled. It cannot always be business first."

I could see by the look on his face that I was getting through to him.

"Tia, I see where I have been absentminded, but why haven't you said anything before this?" he asked gently.

"Mike, if your daughter is on the volleyball team, and they are playing state tournaments, you know how very important that is to her, right? You know you should be there, not just to see her play, but for her, right? It is important for her to see your support. She wants to feel important to you. It is something that you would do because you care, not because she reminds you. It would be utmost on your list because you wouldn't want to hurt her." I finished my little speech, hoping that it all had come out correctly.

"No, I wouldn't. If she didn't tell me, I wouldn't know," he stated, and I could tell he was being truthful.

"Mike, you can't tell me that you don't know what is important to the people you care about!" I said, bewildered. *I guess men really are from Mars*, I thought.

"No, Tia, if people don't tell you, how do you know? You have to tell people what you are thinking or feeling," he said sincerely. I was beginning to understand and learn about the differences between men and women.

That afternoon we talked for hours until we were both starving. We went out hand in hand and shared our "first meal together," as Mike put it. A small café was the closest food, and I couldn't complain; I had been given his complete attention all day. As we prepared to leave, his phone rang, of course, but again, I couldn't complain. I had gotten all I needed.

Mike kissed me gently before dropping me off at the hotel, and he promised to call before I went to bed.

I smiled and said, "I'll hold you to it."

"We both learned a lot today," he said, grinning.

I headed straight for the front desk to pick up that letter. *Yes, we did learn a lot about each other today*, I thought.

CHAPTER 8

My Awakening

*I*t was time to get back to Maui, Sarah, Zoe, and my construction company. Sometimes I wondered whether I was coming or going, and I was getting very tired of living in hotels. Mike and I had talked more about getting an apartment before my next trip.

"All right then," I said, confidently finishing up a staff meeting before I headed back home. "That should be it. Everyone knows the game plan. Are there any questions?"

They all looked at me and shook their heads, looking satisfied regarding their responsibilities.

"Annie, come into my office. I want to speak with you," I said as the others wished me a good trip and dispersed back to their positions.

"Sure, Tia," Annie nervously answered, following me into my office.

She was a tall, blonde, conservatively dressed young lady with soft but striking features. She had been handling the management position very well. She was new to marketing the sale of a spa and had been doing only what was asked of her. It was time for her to take some initiative and use her creativity and imagination.

"Annie, we really need to keep these numbers up on products and show consistent revenue coming in for prospective buyers. Anything you see that can be done starting now will help. I want you to be my eyes. You know the market, and that is why we hired you. I knew it would be difficult when my partner took off, and you are slowly rebuilding our reputation with the spa and our services, but we need to put our heads together and figure out how to engage our clients into using our products at home. I am willing to do what it takes because I want this market! I believe that continued use of the products will only enhance our revenues and eventually attract a buyer."

"The aestheticians and masseurs need extra training on how to sell," she remarked.

I was surprised that Annie was so quick with her remarks. That was good, I thought. She had been thinking about the business.

"They need to inform clients of the added benefits of regularly using the products," she continued. "I will work on that because I believe in them. Is that okay with you?"

"Annie, this is important to me. You don't have to ask. I trust you enough, and please treat this place like it is your own. I want daily numbers now, not biweekly. You and I together will monitor the numbers of the staff. Work out a way to list their sales differently from the front desk. Let's see how it goes, and perhaps they could receive a commission as incentive?" I hoped that she would pick up on my lead.

"Yes, Tia, I understand. Let me work on that. Are you leaving today?" Annie sounded very confident. I was pleased with her response.

"I will be leaving in the morning, but I am busy with a business meeting this evening, unless you have an emergency," I replied. Evening business meetings these days meant Mr. Boss and I were going to be keeping each other warm. I smiled to myself at the thought. "You are doing a great job, Annie. Keep it up," I told her, and then I headed home to the hotel.

><!•>•◦•<•!•<

"Well, hello, mister." I smiled as I open the door to let Mike inside. He instantly put a finger to his lips for me to hush; he was on his phone. I figured I would take advantage of the extra time to make a call to the Big Island that I had been putting off. I stepped into the bathroom for privacy, while he sat on the bed finishing his call. *How romantic. Business always comes first*, I thought.

I finished my call and took another moment to freshen up. This was our last night together, and I wanted to be perfect. I walked into the bedroom to see him already under the covers, ready for me.

"Well, hello again," I said. I was instantly aroused and already desiring this man. Even the thought of him could send me into that thought process, but seeing him ready for me turned the desire up a few notches. How had I gone all these years not having a relationship like this? Or not knowing this kind of relationship existed and what it was all about? For a moment I felt embarrassed about my naïveté.

"Hello," he said in that deep voice of his.

My god, that voice! I retreated quickly to the bathroom.

"Where are you going?" He sounded confused.

"I'll be back," I said. "Give me a minute. Girl stuff." I was sinking back into my shy, nervous self, and I had to talk myself back to the reality of the love we shared. I had to remind myself again that this wasn't dirty or just sex; this was a relationship that was truly formed of two beings who were meant to find one another in this time in their lives. This was beautiful. Sometimes my mind would take me back, and if I hadn't had Mike's eyes to look into, I wouldn't have had the strength to pull myself back out of the closed-off world I had been living in. I thought sometimes that the pressure I put on him or on the relationship wasn't fair. I was sure he felt the pressure but didn't really know where it came from, or he probably blamed it on just my "being a woman." He didn't know what I was going through, and I wasn't going to tell him and risk scaring him off. But I wondered, if we were that close and I felt this much love for him, why would I feel I would be risking it? I wasn't sure. Maybe I just wasn't ready to admit to anyone, even myself, how distant I had made myself to anyone other than my children.

I scolded myself for my behavior—because that was what I had been taught to do. I clicked the lights off on my way back into the room. "Aw," I heard him utter. I was still quite shy. Like many women, I had body issues, and a man like Mr. Boss, I was sure, had been with beautiful women. Even when I was looking my best, I thought my body was anything but beautiful. I liked darkness and covers.

I gently slid into the bed beside him in the darkness, and his strong hands found my waist and pulled me close to him.

"What the hell?" he grumbled a second later, reaching for his phone. "Christ, hello, what is it?" he asked impatiently.

My head spun. *What? You are kidding me. Did he just answer his phone? Yep! Yep, he did.* But I was so into what I was doing, I didn't even stop. If it wasn't an emergency, he would hang up. Sure enough, he hung up.

But his phone rang again. What was going on? He had essentially the same short conversation again and returned his focus to me. But then came yet another ring. I thought if he answered this time, we were going to have to finish later. He must have read my mind because he looked at his phone only long enough to turn it off. I felt important. His phone never got turned off completely. I smiled. No interruptions!

"Now where were we?" he said with a grin as he took hold of my breasts and caressed each of them.

"Right here." We continued our lovemaking, and to our satisfaction, we both climaxed multiple times. But as always, time ran out.

He kissed me gently and said, "I have to go. Sorry."

As he dressed to leave, I gave him my pouty face.

"What's the matter?" he questioned.

"I hate leaving days," I said sadly.

"I'll come by in the morning. What time do you leave?"

"I have to be gone by 6:30 a.m." I winced.

"Okay, then I will come by around six." He kissed me softly on the lips and as always reminded me to lock the door. I closed the door behind him and leaned against it, wishing he didn't leave every night. I heard him on his phone before he got to the end of the hall.

I wondered if I would ever be that last call he made every night.

>─┼─◆─◆─○─◆─◆─┼─<

The sound of my alarm going off was brutal. Five o'clock had come too early when I had been tossing all night, waiting for it to go off. I jumped out of bed, quickly showered, and packed what I hadn't the night before. I was checking on my flight status when he knocked on the door.

I looked at the clock. It was six o'clock sharp. He was right on time. "Hi, you!" I said with a smile as I opened the door.

"Good morning," he said as he put his hand around the back of my neck and pulled me in for a long, passionate kiss. "Do we have time for some love?"

"Well, um ..." I glanced over at the clock. I looked back at his smoldering eyes and wide smile close to my face. I couldn't even respond. I just began to devour his lips.

He steered me into the bedroom. As we passed the light switch, I flicked it off. Shadows danced around the room, and I felt a wave of confidence. I began unbuttoning my blouse as he anxiously took off his shirt and jeans.

"Stay standing," I ordered as I let my skirt and blouse drop to the floor. I was completely nude underneath. "I was expecting you," I whispered.

"Mmm," he said as he lifted my body onto the bed. We were both naked, and already Mike was erect. I rolled on top of him as he easily entered me to find I was already wet with desire. Moving quickly, I climaxed almost instantly, and that sent him into a frenzy.

"Slow, Tia, slow," he gasped, trying to keep control. He grabbed my hips and moved me away from him. "No, no, don't move. Let me ..."

I gave in and let him take control of the movement.

"Feel me deep inside of you. Concentrate and let it take you. Let me take you. Feel it. There you go, baby. Now you got it. Let it go. I got you; let it go. Yes, baby, now you can move. Move however you want."

I felt him shudder beneath me as I gave in to the power of nature.

"C'mon, baby. C'mon underneath me. I want you."

And that was all it took. Another climax came right behind the first one, even before I was underneath him. I watched his face as he succumbed to the pleasure. The emotion was magical as I joined him. Then I heard the words, those special words that every woman waits for.

"I love you, Tia," he whispered.

For some reason I froze. I didn't reply. I think I was in shock. My head spun.

I had to get going. We dressed in a hurry as usual. Between the two of us, someone was always in a hurry.

"Call me when you get to the airport," he instructed.

"I will," I answered as he put my bags in my car.

"Then we'll talk next week about that apartment," he said with a smile, and I drove off to the airport.

> ⊱ ⊰

I checked in, and after getting to my gate, I called him.

"Yes!" he answered smartly. "How was the drive?"

"Uneventful. I could have stayed in bed a bit longer," I teased.

"Yeah, you and me both," he laughed.

We talked a bit about our next move, the spa, and Clare, whom I had grown quite fond of. She was always giving me bits of information on Mr. Boss, which he always denied. I tended to believe him. After all, my employees always thought they knew what I was doing in my private life as well.

"Well, I better get to it. Have a safe flight, Tia, and call when you get in—don't forget!" he stressed.

"Yes, I will. Good-bye," I said slowly.

"Good-bye, Tia."

"Mike?" I quickly said, hoping he hadn't hung up.

"Yes?"

"I love you too," I said quietly.

"I love you. Good-bye."

"Bye."

Soon I boarded the plane, settled in, and closed my eyes. This would be a great flight.

> ⊱ ⊰

The flight arrived on schedule in Maui, and as I neared the baggage claim area, I saw the beautiful faces of my girls.

"Mom, Mom! Over here!" they called out.

"Sarah and Zoe, skipping school again?" I smiled and braced

myself for the two teenagers running to me. "I missed you guys," I said upon impact.

"We have missed you, Mom, and we wanted to surprise you," Sarah said.

We hugged each other and talked nonstop while waiting for my luggage. When my bags flew down the chute, I couldn't hold it in any longer.

"I have lots to tell you. I—we—won't be lugging around all this stuff very soon, and you both may be spending a little more time in New York."

"Please tell us now," Zoe wailed. "Please, Mom, please!"

"Zoe, you are such a baby. I like surprises, and when Mom is ready, she will tell us. Besides, we have something to look forward to because this is sure to be a big surprise—look at her face." Sarah pointed out my broad smile.

"Ha, yes!" Zoe said.

They were content with that, and on the drive home, they told me all that had happened while I was away. They knew that once we arrived home, I would be a zombie for a few days.

It was so good to be home. I took a quick shower and felt a little sad as the last part of Mike's smell on me washed down the drain. I loved his smell. I quickly tried to call him before bed, but there was no answer, as usual. I was exhausted from my trip and the work I had accomplished, not to mention all the physical energy I had been exerting the last few weeks. Before long, I was fast asleep.

I was in a deep sleep when my phone woke me. "Hello," I managed to whisper. I looked at the clock to see it was three thirty.

"Hey, babe."

I heard that voice and was instantly jolted into a panic. I didn't immediately remember where I was. My brain went into overdrive. My god, was my hair a mess? Were my teeth brushed? Oh my, what was I wearing? I gained composure and realized I was in my bed on Maui.

"Where the heck ... are you okay?" I asked.

"Yes," he stated simply, and then he waited for my reply.

"Mike, it is three in the morning. I tried to call you last night."

"Oh my god, I calculated the time difference wrong. I am so sorry. I thought I would be your wake-up call. Sorry. Go back to sleep. Call me when you get up." And he was gone.

Falling back asleep proved impossible. I tossed and turned for an hour before deciding I should get an early start to what would be a crazy day on the Big Island.

Passing all the tourists in the airport was generally a great start to the day. Everyone was in a sunny mood, from the airport staff who were paid to be pleasant to the tourists who were thrilled to be in the tropics. Far from the usual Monday morning office attitudes.

As the plane touched down, I readied myself to hustle to the front to get off before being blocked by the tourists and all their baggage. Not that I generally minded, but this day I was meeting Jack. I had worked with Jack for many years in a consulting capacity. He would be waiting for me curbside. He had no patience, and I knew security had probably made him move at least three times. The Big Island airport was small and had an open-air terminal, but the airport security had to earn their pay, and Jack made them do it for sure.

Just as I got to the curb, Jack passed by in his truck. "Wait! Wait!" I called, flailing my arms. There he went on a mission not to get a ticket from the friendly airport cops. I stood there and waited for him to come back around. My phone rang, and I thought Jack must have seen me too.

"Hey, Jack," I said, as I pressed the button to answer with my Bluetooth.

"Jack? Who the hell is Jack?" barked the familiar gruff voice on the other end.

"I, uh, what? Oh, Mike, I am waiting to be picked up, and I thought this was my ride calling. I just saw him pass by the terminal. I thought he saw me too. Anyway, how are you?"

"Why didn't you call me back this morning?" His tone sounded accusatory.

"What? Well … I had to get to the airport and had calls to make." I stopped myself. "Just busy with work," I said.

"Tia!" This time it was Jack calling out to me in a gruff voice. Great, this was going to be a good day. Testosterone Monday! I laughed to myself. Jack was motioning to the airport cop who was standing at attention, waiting to pounce. I sped up my pace to make it to the pickup while finishing my conversation with Mr. Boss.

"I will call you tonight on my way back to Maui. Is that good?" I asked.

"I will be in meetings tonight. Call me in the morning, please," Mr. Boss said.

"Will do, sir!" I said matter-of-factly, still a little ticked. I hung up, but in spite of my prissiness, I thought, *There was that "please" again. What guy says that? Oh yeah, that's right, dare I say my guy!*

Jack and I made it out of the airport with no incident. We spent the next few hours at the job site going over the progress made and discussing the delivery delays. I held a meeting and organized how to optimize production schedules to prevent Jack the financial loss. We left, and Jack was satisfied with a newfound confidence in his development project.

<hr>

"Hey, I was just about to call you," I said, answering my phone.

"Where are you?" Mike asked.

"I am almost to the airport, headed back to Maui."

"When will you be home?"

"About five."

"Will you be alone?"

"Well, yes," I said, a little confused. "I will be at the house. I'm sure the girls are busy with work or friends. Why?" It felt like he was having jealousy issues. If this was going to escalate, we would need to talk.

"Okay, call me when you get to your house and get settled. I want to—no, need to—talk to you about something critical."

Oh boy, I thought, *is this another man thing? Does he think he owns me now? Am I going to get scolded for riding around with another man?* I pushed the thought out of my head and tried to put those past confrontations behind me. This was a different relationship with a totally different man, I told myself.

"Hmm, okay. Can I at least know what we are going to be talking about? I'd like to be prepared," I said, trying to sound more businesslike.

"Oh, you won't need to be prepared." I could tell he was smiling.

My thoughts ran away. So was he surprising me with something? What could it be? I knew he wasn't there.

I quickly made my way out of the airport and to my car. The anticipation was making me crazy. I called the girls and found out their plans for the evening. I learned that both would be busy till late. My curiosity was aroused, and I quickly pulled up Mike's number so I could be ready to call as soon as I pulled into my garage.

But when I called, the line was busy. What the heck? I got out and ran into the house, pushing send again on my way. This time it went through.

"Hello," he said in that gruff, no-nonsense voice.

"Hello. What is with your phone? It just rang busy. Whose phone rings busy these days?"

"My phone has the radio feature; it rings busy when I'm on the radio," he explained.

"Oh," I said. I didn't really care. "I was just wondering what was so darn important that we needed to talk in private tonight."

"Have you forgotten the apartment?"

"No. I'm sorry. Is that what we needed to discuss?"

"No." I heard a faint laugh on the other end of the line.

"Why are you laughing?" I blurted out. I then realized I sounded like a ten-year-old. "Mike, please, I'm nervous about us and, I guess, sensitive. Don't mess with my head."

"I'm not messing with you. I would never mess with you. I just hope you would never mess with me. I can't stand the thought of another man thinking he could be with you. I love you. Do you miss me, baby? Do you long for me? Do you want me?"

This was new. Of course, I would never be with another man. I thought he should've known that, although we hadn't clarified our relationship. Maybe this was his way of doing that. He had definitely quickly become the person I would do anything for.

"Of course, I want you, babe. Where is all this coming from?" I asked, feeling a little confused and also becoming aroused.

"I just miss you so much sometimes. I want to feel you beneath me," he blurted out.

"Oh, babe, I miss you too. I'm so sorry we are so far apart."

"Are you wet?" he asked.

"What?" I was confused.

"You heard me. Are you … do you want me? If you close your eyes right now, can you feel me beside you?"

I heard him breathe in deeply, waiting for my response. I was breathing deeply as well. Part of me wanted to let him know that he had all of me, that he'd had all of me from the first kiss on that cold sidewalk when he told me I was beautiful. Another part of me was still scared.

Did he know then the responsibility of my heart and soul that he held? Did he know the gravity of this young heart and how he could destroy it with one word? Did he know how many times he had brought me to tears and how much he meant to me—his heart, soul, mind, and body? Oh yes, that body!

"Hello, you there?" he said.

"Oh yes, I'm here, and how dare you tease like this, six thousand miles away, knowing there is nothing we can do about it?" I said naively.

"Oh, baby, I would never tease you that badly. Why don't you get naked? Because I am, and I am hard as a rock waiting for you."

"What? Wait … what?" I was stunned. "Okay, phone sex. I have only heard of this, babe. Ah … this may not go as you planned," I said honestly, already a little embarrassed.

"Oh, hon. With you it is an adventure worth every twist, believe me."

"Okay, here goes," I said, putting the phone on speaker.

"Just be vocal. I want to hear you. I want to hear everything," he said, encouraging me.

"Okay, baby, I want to tell you everything. I am ready. Talk to me. Lead me through this; love me virtually," I said. I knew I needed to feel my lover; I knew I couldn't lose this bond we had, and I couldn't risk him thinking I was getting it somewhere else. "Baby, I'm wet and waiting for you." I stumbled on my words, but the words were true—wet I was and oh so ready. The minute he had said he was hard as a rock, I could feel that sensation and knew it wouldn't be long before I would reach a climax.

"Okay," he said, his soft voice penetrating my very soul.

My mind was racing. *Will I do this right? What do I say? Will I sound silly?*

Suddenly, he broke the silence, almost as if he was reading my mind. "Babe, let yourself go," he instructed. "Just relax and let me take over; if all I hear is you breathing, that's all I need this time. I just want you to enjoy yourself. Let me know I can please you."

Oh my god, those words, that voice. He got me going without a touch. How could this be? Were our souls connected, or was he just that good? I struggled with my brain. *Calm down, relax, breathe, and let Mike hear how much you care*, I told myself.

"Babe, you with me?" he questioned, sounding a little concerned.

"Yes, yes, I'm here."

"You must be so beautiful right now. I want you to close your eyes and move your hands down your body like I would. Feel your breasts on the way past; feel how soft and round they are, how warm your body is becoming. Move your hand down the small part of your waist; feel what I feel when I make love to you, feel how beautiful you are … How are you doing, love?"

"Oh my god, I think I am about to climax already," I said, not even believing I had just said that on the phone. I could tell he was smiling, and that turned me on even more.

"Anything you want to tell me?" he said, almost begging.

"Yes, baby. Can I touch myself now?" I said softly, almost embarrassed.

"Oh yes, baby, I am already there myself. I want to hear you moan just like you do when I am inside you. Let me hear you. Move your hand down your body and gently massage yourself … that's right, baby. Oh god, you are going to make me finish before I want to. I can hear the pleasure in your breath. Let me hear your voice. I want to hear your voice."

"Oh god, babe, I am really wet. I want you inside of me so badly right now." I couldn't think of anything else to say. I just let Mother

Nature take over my body and let my voice be heard. I could hear my-self almost as if from another room. I faintly heard him on the other end, as we reached the ultimate goal at the same time.

"Holy shit," he gasped, "that was amazing."

I smiled that satisfied smile and felt my body come back down to the bed. Yes, that had been pretty great. Who would have thought?

"We were amazing," I said.

"I just have to get you to talk a little bit more, maybe a little dirty ... we'll get there. We have forever," he said.

"Well, my teacher was pretty amazing, and I am enjoying the lessons. That was incredible, Mike. Have you ever done that before?" I instantly regretted asking. Maybe I wasn't ready for his answer.

"No, I have not," he said. "I can hear the birds singing; it must be about sunset."

"Yes, my pets."

"Speaking of pets, do your kids have any?" he asked.

"No, I have a few really good excuses every time they ask, such as we travel too much. But if I admit it, the truth is I know I would get too attached, and I never want to say good-bye to something I love. I know that sounds kinda silly. I just hate being sad, and I don't ever want to put my kids through that either." I thought about how selfish I sounded.

"No, that's not silly at all. I remember when our dog died. My daughter must have been about ten. I watched her through the kitchen window putting flowers on his grave, tears streaming down her face. I had tried to console her earlier, but nothing helped. I could see and feel her pain. Between knowing there was nothing I could do or say to console her and feeling my own pain of the loss, I vowed we would never again have a pet."

"That sounds rough. Exactly my point," I said.

"We all have our stories, right?" he said, trying to lighten the conversation.

"I would have never guessed you to be such a softy after seeing you in the business world and interacting with your employees with such authority."

"I have to keep up the tough exterior. You know, I can't let people get to know me too well. I think I am beginning to get to know another person like that. I think you may know her quite well." I could hear the smile in his voice. "Listen, I better get some sleep. I love you, sweetheart," he said softly.

I smiled. He had never called me sweetheart. "I love you too. Talk to you tomorrow."

I hung up the phone and set it beside me on the bed. I did not want to move and disturb that feeling of contentment in my entire body.

The warm orange glow of the sunset streamed through my windows. I could hear the birds singing good night to one another and felt the cool ocean breeze wash over my body. My body had never felt so comfortable, my mind had never been this still, and my heart had never felt so full. I wanted to remember this moment forever.

"Hey, Mom," a squeaky little voice called from downstairs, "are you in bed?"

"Hey, Zoe. I'm upstairs. Just getting ready to shower. Got home a little late. How was your day?" I called down.

"Oh, ya know, I'm going to take a swim and then hit the hay. You want to swim with me, please?" she begged.

Zoe hated to swim alone, so I trudged down the stairs. I knew that halfway into the swim, we would be laughing and enjoying ourselves, even though right then I just wanted to be thinking about the phone call I had just finished.

The next morning I awoke with a plan. If it was dirty talk Mr. Boss wanted, it was dirty talk Mr. Boss was going to get. I was a firm believer in continuing education. I guessed this was no different. So I researched how to talk dirty to your man, and it turned out there were many people who wanted to teach just that. I bought my first book and hoped that by the time the subject came up again, I could surprise Mr. Bossy.

CHAPTER 9

Home Away from Home

During the next week I spent more time than usual with the girls. So when I had a moment, I was anxious to call Mike.

"Hello," he answered.

"It's a great Monday, isn't it?" I chirped.

"Well, mine is almost over, but it was pretty good," Mr. Boss said jokingly.

"I know this time difference is for the birds. Well, I'm glad yours was good. Mine is going to be good too. I will call you this afternoon before you go to bed."

"Actually, I have a meeting tonight, but I will try to call you after. I have some good news, though. I have a vacancy at one of the apartment complexes next month for you and the girls. How does that sound?"

"That sounds great, Mike." I was shocked and couldn't believe this was happening. I became nervous. "You do understand I have to be here most of the time, though, right? I just want to be up front about that—my construction company and the girls' school and all." I found myself already making excuses.

"Calm down. You don't have to worry. It will be okay. Small steps, Tia, small steps." I could tell that he was smiling. God, I loved that smile. He knew just the right thing to say to me, and I loved that too. "I have to get going. I'll call you soon."

"Yeah, me too. I love you—do you know that?" he asked.

"Oh, Mike, you make me really happy. I love *you*!" I exclaimed, beaming.

⊱ ⊰⊱ ⊙ ⊰⊱ ⊰

I drove to my office, and after a few hours of catching up on all the news, problems, and job schedules, I finally relaxed with a cup of coffee. I somehow always thought of that first meeting at Mike's golf course when I drank morning coffee. I sat at my desk daydreaming. I really did love this man, for what he stood for, for his smile, his eyes, his manner, his mind, for the chemistry between us, for his hands, for his body, for his mind-blowing sex, for ...

"Tia!" My thoughts were suddenly interrupted.

"Yes? Huh, yes?" I stuttered.

"Oh my god, did you not hear the phone ringing a zillion times?" My office assistant could be over the top sometimes, but yes, I was daydreaming a lot lately, especially during my first few days of being home from New York.

"Well, are you going to answer, or shall I pick up and tell them you are still in New York? It certainly seems that way," she said with a scowl.

"I got it, I got it," I said while wondering if I should be upset with her or just take the beating.

"Good Monday morning," I sang. "This is Tia." My usual greeting hadn't changed. I was just a little more preoccupied these days. Maybe I *should've* taken a few extra private phone calls with Mr. Boss.

"Tia, this is Jack Smith on the Big Island."

"Hey, Jack. What can I do for you?"

"Tia, I seem to have encountered a problem with the county on that development in Ocean Estates. Seems they think they own all the lava down there," he said in a half-joking manner.

Jack was a heck of a guy, but whenever he called, I knew it would take at least a day or so of work to remedy whatever problem had come about. Jack was aware that I was in the know and could handle any fallout. Therefore, I was the first person he unloaded his problems on.

"Jack, you know I own all that lava down there. What the heck are they crossing that line for? Those county boys don't want to mess with you and me. We'll shake them up, and they'll be praying to Pele, the Hawaiian volcano goddess, for forgiveness," I said, laughing.

That got a small chuckle out of him. "But seriously, Tia, we need to sit down and discuss this. I have half my fortune invested in this development, and if they delay it, I'm screwed. I need a little help here."

"Okay, Jack. Send me over the information they have sent you, and I will take a look this afternoon. It can't be too bad. I'm sure they are just ruffling feathers. It'll be okay. Meanwhile, I need you to look at those plans for the Saddle Road project."

"All right, when do you need them?"

"We are set to start in three weeks. I still haven't seen the final scope," I explained.

"Yup, let's talk about it Friday at the Pau Hana party. I'll buy you a drink."

"Sounds great!" But he would not be buying me a drink because they were all free at the Pau Hana party, which was just a Friday night get-together. I wondered what Mike would've thought about another guy buying me a drink.

>—⊹—◦—⊹—⊰

Four weeks later

It was Sunday night, and I had planned a nice relaxing dinner for the girls and me. I had decided that it was time for me let them in on the plans for New York. I had also decided it was time to lose those seven pounds that had been hanging around too long and maybe start hitting the gym a little more because I noticed some things heading south. My goal was to be comfortable enough with myself the next time I was in New York that I could give my man a sensual striptease act, though I would still need the candlelight confidence, of course. I couldn't believe I was even thinking like this; I was becoming a new woman. This Sunday night dinner with the girls would be my last splurge for a while. Suddenly, my thoughts were interrupted.

"Why are we eating pasta, Mom?" exclaimed Zoe. "I mean … I don't mind, but since when do you eat pasta as a main dish?"

"I know, I know," I said. "I am starting a new eating regimen tomorrow, and I know I won't get pasta for a while," I explained with a devilish grin.

Sarah was running late, so we sat down without her, and Zoe told me all about her week ahead before Sarah got home.

I had waited the entire week to tell them about the New York apartment. I didn't know whether they would be excited or upset. They had grown so much the last year, and leaving their boyfriends and girlfriends for a few weeks at a time might be more than they want.

"Well, hello, Sarah. Nice of you to join in," I said when she finally arrived. I was teasing but also a little annoyed that she was so late.

"I'm sorry. I was running late, and then Jake wanted to grab pizza, and I couldn't say no to him," she said, gushing.

"What?" Zoe almost yelled. "Jake? You were late to Sunday dinner for Jake?" She slid her chair back and removed Sarah's plate. "You won't be needing this then, will you, missy?" she said, quite snippy.

"Whatever, Zoe. You're just jealous," Sarah quipped.

"Oh goodness, girls. Let's be nice. Please, it's Sunday, and I do have some exciting news I wanted to talk about," I said, hoping the news wouldn't bring more anguish to the already stormy dinner. "You know I spend a lot of time in New York these days. And the spa needs more and more of my time. If I am going to make this work out there, I need to commit to lengthier stays, so—"

Sarah interrupted me. "Hold on, Zoe. Here it comes. You might be pleased that she waited."

"Oh, hush up, Sarah," said Zoe.

"What would you say if I got an apartment out there? A place we could hang our hats, so to speak, for a month or so at a time and not worry about packing and unpacking every time?" I decided to keep talking. "We could all be together more when I do have to be there." I saw blank stares. "Well, what do you think?"

I knew a year ago they would have loved the idea, but so much had changed in their little worlds and so fast. I wasn't sure about the reaction I was going to get, and the longer the silence continued, the more nervous I got. What if they hated the idea, and I had to tell Mike I wouldn't be seeing him more often after all? My girls did come first, and he knew that, but what if we actually had to face that? My head spun for what seemed like forever before they finally answered me.

Squeals were all I heard. Then they began hugging and high-fiving. The little tiff was over. The boy who had made Sarah late for dinner was long forgotten, and they were best friends again! *Okay, this is good,* I thought.

"This is great!" I said aloud. I stood up and did an animated dance, my arms flailing.

They both giggled and joined me in our happy dance.

"This is awesome. Now we are bicoastal kids," said Zoe.

"Oh yeah, this is cool," Sarah agreed. We all sat back down.

"Well, I guess you're in then? I was a little concerned you wouldn't want to be leaving your island home for long periods of time. You know you will start to miss it, right?" I let them know in my own way that they wouldn't be jet-setting every other week.

"How long do we have to stay away?" Zoe quickly sounded concerned.

"Well, I don't know, but to make it worth the trip, at least a few weeks at a time." I realized that Mike and I would want alone time, so I followed up by saying, "But for a good balance you can stay at home yourselves, like you do now, for a week or so on either end of the trip. We will work it out." I finished my last few bites and stood up to clear the table.

"Two-bedroom or three-bedroom, Mom? 'Cause you know how messy Sarah is, right?" Zoe complained as she grabbed her dishes and headed toward the sink.

"Oh, I am not listening to complaints about that while we are in New York. It will be a three-bedroom for sure!"

We all pitched in with the after-dinner chores and chitchatted about what our New York life would be like and how much fun we would have on the weekends when we could spend time in the city. I wondered what they would think if they knew about Mike, if they knew their mom had someone who made her so very happy.

"Oh my god. I am so full," Zoe said, puffing her cheeks out like a chipmunk with nuts in her mouth.

"Who is hitting the gym in the morning with me?" I said loudly.

"Me for sure!" Zoe answered. Sarah just rolled her eyes.

The next morning, my phone rang early. "Good Monday morning." That familiar voice vibrated through my earpiece and straight through my body.

"Good afternoon, Mike. What time is it there?" I questioned.

"It is one fifteen," he answered. "How was your weekend?" He sounded like he was in a great mood, and I was about to make it even better.

"My weekend was great as usual. I missed talking to you, but I did talk to the girls about the apartment." I waited for a response.

"Oh yeah, what did they say?" I could tell he was on edge. "Well?" he asked again.

I held out a little bit just for fun.

"Tia, did you hear me? Well, what is the verdict?"

I began to laugh. "They are super excited, Mike. I don't think they'll be staying more than three or so weeks at a time. That will be good for us. We still need to keep us under wraps, at least until we figure us out."

"Of course. I still have my divorce and financial legal issues to settle too. Wouldn't want to mess that up by coming forward now. So this is good." He sounded relieved and pleased. "I will get the furniture ready to go. Let's do this, Tia. I feel like a young man again."

"Really? What would a young man do with this young woman right now?" I teased.

"You really are turning into quite the little vixen, aren't you?" he said, sounding almost surprised. "Just as long as I keep you satisfied, baby, and I'm the only place you're getting it, that's all I care about." He had quickly turned my innocent tease serious.

"You know it, babe. You are all I think about," I assured him.

>─┼─◆─┼─○─┼─◆─┼─<

The next four weeks flew by, and before I knew it, I was headed to New York to settle into our new apartment.

"Girls, we have to bring our warmest clothes, and I am telling you now, there is no way I can prepare you for how chilly it will be in the evening and night. So bundle up, and we will spend the first few days shopping for warm clothes once you get there."

"Okay, Mom, we will," Sarah called back. "See, I told you, Zoe. You never listen to me, do you?"

"Hey, girls, stop fighting," I said as I walked into Sarah's room. "Since I'm leaving a week ahead of you, I am sure you will be doing nothing but studying, right? I am going to miss my little angels so very much, but I will see you in nine days." We all had a group hug. They helped me finish packing, and then I was off to the airport.

>—!—>—•—O—•—<—!—<

I already missed my girls, and I was only one hour into the eleven-and-a-half-hour flight. It was bittersweet. I knew they missed me too, but part of me knew they would relish their free time. They were growing up so fast, and soon I would be wondering what I was going to do without them. On the other hand, every time I heard those cabin doors close, and I was bound for New York, I would get butterflies, knowing that soon I would be with Mike.

⇢☞ CHAPTER 10 ☜⇠

Lost in Love

There you are, I thought, smiling to myself. Mike was waiting for me outside the gate. Those brown eyes never ceased to light up my world. He smiled and reached for me.

"Oh, Tia, I have missed you." He held me close and nuzzled into my hair. "I wish I could take you right here. I wish I could kiss you like I want."

"Me too." I giggled as I pulled away. To the general public we were still just business colleagues and friends, so the greetings were friendly to the onlooker, although I couldn't recall ever holding a friend quite that tight or for that long.

"Are you hungry?" he asked as he put my bags in the trunk.

"Are you kidding? Don't you know by now, after that flight, I just need to get to bed?"

"Yeah, you and me both," he quickly teased back, climbing into the car and putting his hand high on my thigh.

"Oh, you are too funny. I'm so fuzzy right now, I can't even think straight. I would probably fall asleep on you." I put my hand on his.

"That's okay. I can take care of business until you wake up," he said, continuing with the teasing.

After traveling for that long with no sleep, not to mention the time zone change, my brain was barely functioning. The usual banter was not going as planned, not that we made too many plans. We just tried to get as much of each other as we could in the little time we had together—we had mastered that!

We drove to the apartment in silence. I rested my eyes while holding his hand. Whenever I would look over at him, he smiled lovingly and gave me that look I had become accustomed to. I couldn't help but touch his face.

"I have missed that smile, Mike," I whispered.

We pulled into the apartment parking lot and immediately released our hands when we noticed a few employees standing outside. How I hated that and wished we could just be us, no matter where we were or who we were with.

"Hey," Mike bellowed, opening his door, "I thought you guys were supposed to be spraying unit thirty-six today? What the hell are you doing down here?"

"Sheet rockers have us held up, so Joe sent us down here to get some of the cleanup finished at this place." They didn't seem at all rattled by the harshness of Mike's tone. I guessed they were used to it.

Being in an apartment complex was not really like being home, not that I wanted it to be. Simply, it wasn't what I was used to.

While I unloaded my suitcases, he attended to his "unruly" employees. *Poor guys*, I thought, *they're just doing their job.* On the other hand, I knew how it went. There were some people who needed to be lined out every hour, or every minute for that matter, or they would be chasing butterflies around the field.

"Here, let me get that." Mike caught up to me just as I hit the door of the apartment. "Leave these here and let me show you around—a quick tour!"

Hmm, that was all I needed. I tried to be enthusiastic. It was nice. The pool was heated, thank goodness. My mind took off back to the islands. I thought about my midnight swims and how beautiful it was to see the moon dance off the ocean. That did sound a little like a cliché, but it was true. When the waves rippled in under the moonlight, the light appeared to be dancing off the water. The ripples would shimmer in such a way that it couldn't be described as anything other than dance.

"What are you thinking?"

"Oh, nothing, just tired and taking it all in. Sorry I'm not more energetic," I said as I went back to my daydream. Sunsets were so colorful. And then there was the sound of the waves crashing on the rocks outside my bedroom window, lulling me to sleep every night. But of course, I didn't have Mr. Boss there; he made up for all the things I missed about home.

Back at the apartment door, he tried to pick up my bag. "I got it!" I said, almost sternly. "I'm sorry," I said immediately. "I'm just tired and need some sleep."

He took my bags in. "Why don't you find your way to the bed, and I'll stop back in a few hours. How's that sound?" He smiled.

"That sounds great. I'll see you then."

He kissed me gently, and I smiled as I watched his masculine frame head toward the door. After he closed the door behind him, I headed straight for the bedroom. It seemed he knew what I liked—there were numerous down pillows and a nice white down comforter on a king-size bed. I smiled as I thought about what would be taking place in this bed very soon.

><!◆>•O•<◆>!◁

I awoke to a dark, silent room. Confused at my surroundings, I questioned where I was. Oh yes, I was in New York! It hadn't hit me immediately because it was dark and not cold. I heard the hum of the heat register. Maybe I had turned it on while sleepwalking. *What time is it?* I wondered as I reached for my phone. Great, my phone was dead. I looked at the clock on the nightstand. *It can't be,* I thought. Mike was going to kill me. It was already ten. I must have slept through his call, or my phone died before he called.

I fell asleep again waiting for my phone to charge and didn't wake until morning. When I awoke again, I was still not refreshed, but I knew I needed to call Mike. I grabbed my phone and saw it was it was nine thirty in the morning. I couldn't believe how long I had slept. It did usually take me three to four days until I felt completely like myself again. I groggily dialed his number.

"Well, good morning."

Good, he isn't mad, I thought. "I am so sorry I didn't call you last night. I didn't even wake up till after ten. Then my phone was dead. I was going to—"

"It's okay, Tia. I knew you were tired. I came over and turned on the heat for you."

"What? I didn't even hear you. How come you didn't wake me up?" I asked.

"You didn't even wriggle when I put a blanket over you, so I decided not to bother you."

"I wish you would have," I said, mad at myself for being crabby yesterday.

"Well, I didn't want to startle you and have you screaming. You would wake up the neighbors, and we don't want my buddies the cops over here. How would that look?" he said with a laugh.

"Yes, you're right, but I don't think I would have screamed; you could have always muffled my mouth," I suggested.

"Hmm, so you're rested, I take it?"

"Well, not completely myself, but I am better than yesterday."

"I'll see you in about two hours. How does that sound?"

"Perfect!" I answered before I remembered that I had made plans to meet with Annie at the spa. Oh well, Mike was more important these days, and Annie would be working the late shift anyway. I would call her as soon as I showered and got my things organized.

I was quick to get things arranged so that I could concentrate totally on Mike when he arrived. Three hours passed with no phone call. I knew how much he missed me and wanted to see me, so I thought something must have come up. I waited another hour and then decided to go ahead and see Annie. I was getting ready to leave when Mike knocked. With files and jacket in hand, I opened the door.

"Hey, you. You're not skipping town on me, are you?" He smiled.

I knew he was referencing the "Dear John" letter I had tried to leave at the hotel before. I wasn't sure if it was an attempt at humor or if he was feeling a little insecure. I sometimes thought that in his own small way, he might be a little unsure of himself, but I was quickly turned back to reality when his business edge came into play, or when he would confidently pull me into his arms, taking me to magical places.

"No, not skipping town this time," I stated coldly, hoping he got the hint. For some reason I was unable to let him know when he hurt my feelings or when I felt uncomfortable around him. I knew the long talk we'd had should have erased all of that insecurity. I thought more about how as an abused child I had been taught to not speak up and to hide all my feelings, to be completely submissive; the message was that I didn't matter. I knew Mike didn't know what was going on in my mind, and I felt bad for the way I would snap instead of explain what I was thinking. I knew I had to start dealing with these built-up anxieties, and I had to stop putting our relationship through this if we were going to move forward. I had to communicate.

But he also had to stop forgetting time and start remembering when I was waiting. I didn't like waiting around for a guy that I had been longing for, for weeks. I had been there almost two days, and we hadn't made love yet! Something was very odd about that. He had plenty of time to get his ducks in a row so that we could have some alone time. Then I stopped myself—maybe he had set aside yesterday afternoon when I was sleeping. I had to stop analyzing. Maybe it was just the jet lag.

"Something wrong?" he asked, looking puzzled.

"No," I lied again. "I have to meet Annie. I was supposed to go earlier, but I waited for you … now, I really have to get down there." I thought I sounded self-assured.

"Oh, okay, sorry. I got held up with my accountant. You know how those guys are." He smiled.

It's a good thing he smiles at me a lot, I thought. *God, that smile.* I couldn't wait to feel his lips on mine, to take in his breath as he held me tight. I was daydreaming about him, and he was right here in front of me.

"What are you smiling at, Tia? You are acting strange."

"You!" I said bravely. "When do you suppose that we are finally going to get our hands on each other?" I said, gathering my car keys from my jacket pocket, not wanting to look at him. "Mike, this time,

I have to leave! I need to get my rear to the spa, sorry," I said, still not looking at him as I opened the door.

"All right, then how about seven tonight? You going to be rested enough?" he said from behind me.

"Sure will," I said flippantly. I was trying not to show how disappointed I was that he hadn't even called. He just thought he could stop by, and I would be willing, ready, and waiting! I had let this behavior continue, so I couldn't be too mad at him. I turned to him, tired of pretending. "I will see you at seven, no later, all right?" I was serious.

He didn't answer, but just grinned and pulled away.

CHAPTER 11

The Spa in Trouble

"Tia, it is so good to see you," Annie said, greeting me with a genuine hug.

I hugged her back and then pulled out the chocolate macadamia nuts and Kona coffee that I always brought. She accepted them graciously.

"Now, this is why I love you," she joked.

"Sorry I took so long," I said. I realized that I hadn't offered an excuse. I shouldn't have had to. I was the boss. Why didn't I do that with Mike?

I had learned a lot from watching Mr. Boss, both good and bad. Of course, I learned from everyone, even my kids. I always told them, "You never know everything, and you can learn every day from someone, even if it is just reminding you of something that you forgot. Be grateful to the person for giving you a gift of knowledge and treat them accordingly. We must rule with our hearts." I wondered to myself if that was my problem. When I ruled with my heart, it got stomped on—a lot. But I couldn't imagine being any other way. I did need to learn to speak up more to balance it out. Yes, that was it! Balance, not change—balance!

Annie interrupted my thoughts. I only heard the tail end of what she was explaining. "And then he said he's not paying for the service. I gladly took it off the bill and deleted him out of the system. I then let everyone know he's not welcome back. What do you think, Tia? Was I wrong?"

You have to pay attention to business and stop occupying your mind with Mr. Boss, I scolded myself.

"No, not at all, Annie. That is what you are being paid to do. Make decisions like that and stand by them. Always alert the employees, notify me, and move on. You don't have to question if it's right or wrong; it's done … I will tell you if you have made a decision that I don't feel was justified," I told her, trying to sound like I had listened to the entire story. I did feel that Annie was doing a good enough job, and she didn't need a babysitter. I tried to bolster her confidence every chance I got; if there was any fault in her, it was lack of confidence.

I was looking over the numbers when I heard a wonderful, soft, familiar voice. It was Mike's assistant, Clare.

"Well, hello," I said, smiling softly as I came out from around the counter to give her a hug.

"It is so great to see you," Clare said, looking sincerely happy to see me. "I thought you would have come by the office. Mike said you were in town," she said.

"Oh, I was planning on coming by tomorrow or on the weekend. Just busy. You know how it is."

"I know. I think you work harder than Mike. You two would have made the perfect couple," she said, grinning suspiciously.

I wondered if she knew, but why wouldn't she just ask?

"I think we would've killed each other," I said with a smile, trying to act nonchalant about the comment. "The girls will be in next week, so I am trying to get things settled a little," I said.

"You must bring them by so I can say at least say hi!"

"Of course I will. They enjoyed the lunch they had with you."

"Do you want to get some dinner later with me?"

"Yes, that would be great. I am hungry, being off my entire time schedule. How about we get some sushi?"

I knew that wasn't the local cuisine, but there was a small sushi place in the shopping plaza, and it was quick. I didn't want to be late for Mr. Boss since I had been adamant about his being on time.

She smiled. "I guess just for you, I could do sushi, but you're going to have to school me on the correct way to eat it." She then quickly mentioned that she had a meeting for the golf tournament that night and couldn't be late.

"Sure, we can eat quickly," I said, relieved that she wouldn't want to linger and gossip. We set a time, and Clare left.

I spent the next hour going through the books, and very soon it was time for me to get going. I noticed how busy the spa was when I left and nodded in relief to myself. "Annie, I am taking off now. I will see you later," I called on my way out.

I was a bit disappointed in Annie after going through the numbers and realizing she hadn't been sending me the correct numbers like I had asked. The numbers for the spa were much lower than I had thought. My stomach wasn't quite ready for sushi, but I would fake it. I smiled as I reminded myself how expert I had become at putting on a good face.

The sushi place was pretty slow because of the time and day. Clare and I picked a window booth. We laughed and kidded each other throughout the meal. I taught her, or at least I tried to teach her, how to use chopsticks and how to peel the nori from the roll since I didn't like the seaweed, but it was too hard for a beginner to gracefully peel sticky rice from a sticky seaweed wrap.

"Don't try to save too much of the rice," I instructed her. "There's always another piece." She accepted my giggly criticism, and we agreed about how much we had missed each other.

"Oh, Tia, it is good to laugh. It has been so stressful around the office, and my personal life is … well, I think I'm headed for divorce."

I knew she wanted to talk, but I also knew we had limited time.

"What about the girls?" she quickly inquired, trying to change the subject as if she had said something wrong.

"The girls … where do I start? Zoe has made the all-state national finals in hockey, and so has Sarah, but they are in different groups this year for age. I'll be traveling for two months as a hockey mom this year instead of one month. They are excited, but I am stressing … it's hard not to let them know how much I worry."

"I can't imagine the job you have, dealing with two spirited young ladies."

"With everything else going on, I want them to know they are still, and always will be, number one. Well, unless I meet that handsome man who will sweep me off my feet and take me into fantasy land ..." I laughed. Little did she know I had already met that man, and I was well on my way to fantasy land with him. It would've been nice to be able to tell someone. I wished I had at least one girlfriend to confide in.

As we drank our sake, the conversation turned to the spa, and I found her to be very interested. So I continued on, telling her about the plans for a buyer.

"Yes, I know Mike would love to have that kind of business make it in his shopping center," Clare said. "It really adds class and ..." Clare's cell phone rang before she could finish the thought. Looking at the screen, she said, "Tia, I have to take this. It's Mike. Promise you won't eat that last wonton." She smiled and headed for the door.

"I promise," I said, nodding to her.

While she was gone, I asked for the check and gave my credit card. We needed to get going. I glanced outside to see Clare standing on the edge of the parking area, kicking rocks and looking around. I wondered if Mike knew we were having dinner. The private phone call took almost fifteen minutes.

"I saved the last wonton for you to take home," I sang out as I lifted up the doggie bag upon her return. "What took you so long, and why so secret?" I asked, trying to hide the annoyance I felt.

"Well, you know Mike. He's intense and needs answers ... like *now!*"

I might need some answers too, I thought. My jealous mind got carried away as we exited the restaurant and headed for our cars. I mulled over our conversation in my head. Was Clare actually enjoying our newfound friendship, or was she trying to get information? I knew we had become friends. It just seemed our conversations were always centered around the spa or Mike. But it was nice to have someone to talk to. I guessed if Mike trusted her, then I could too.

Clare interrupted my thoughts. "Tia, when do you leave? Now don't forget to bring the girls by," she said so sweetly.

"Of course I will, and we will have lunch again, next time on you!" I joked.

She laughed as she closed her car door. *Running off to Mr. Boss!* I thought.

⤜┤◆▸•○•◂◆├⤛

I rushed back to the apartment. Just as I noticed I was going well over the speed limit, I saw the police lights in my rearview mirror. *Oh my god!* I thought. *I have never had a speeding ticket. Are you kidding me? I just broke my record, twenty-something years of perfect driving. Oh well.*

"Hello, miss," the officer said politely

"Hello." I tried to sound calm, cool, and collected.

I began imagining how fast I must have been going and how much it was going to cost me, and I wondered whether the rental car company would ever rent to me again.

"Did you know your back right blinker is out?" the policeman said.

"Huh, what? You mean I wasn't speeding?"

"No, ma'am. I just need to see your license, registration, and insurance."

Phew! I handed over my license as I started to explain that this was a rental car.

"Tia, from Hawaii! Why didn't you say so? How the hell are you? What are you doing here? Why didn't I know you were here?"

I was caught off-guard by the barrage of questions. "I, uh, don't know ..."

"It's me, Jimmy," he said while he pulled off his police cap.

I saw the bald head and knew immediately that this was the guy who had saved my butt a few times. Once when a woman had hit me in a snowstorm, and I was dumb enough to believe she would give me her information in a phone call later, he had helped me track her down and supply the car rental agency with her information so that I wasn't stuck with the bill. He had also helped me in a possible lawsuit with the spa, doing investigative-type work. I guess Mr. Boss having connections with the state troopers had worked out well for me too.

"Hey, Jimmy. How are you?"

"Well, apparently better than you. I mean, a rental company that gives you a car with rear signal lights out is not so good."

I laughed. "Oh, Jimmy, if you only knew. That is the least of my worries."

"Well, since the spa business is so stressful, why don't you get massages every day?" he questioned as if he were Mr. Boss.

"I wish it were that easy," I retorted.

"Okay, maybe we can have a glass of wine after work some night. How long are you in town?"

"About a month. My daughters will be here next week. Maybe a pizza and wine with them?" I suggested, knowing he would get the hint. I knew about Jimmy. He was definitely not in for the long-term thing, and he was definitely not in the running with me.

"Huh, yeah, sure. Give me a call then. I'll be seeing you." Smiling, he added, "Get going, and let the rental company know about the lights ... and as for you, keep the speed down."

I smiled. "Thanks, Jimmy," I said as I slowly pulled away.

I was not sure whether I'd gotten off on my own or because Mr. Boss had friends in high places or, in this case, the state police office.

CHAPTER 12

Insanity

*D*riving into the cul-de-sac parking, I did not see Mr. Boss. I scurried out of my car and into my apartment. This would give me time to get freshened up and light some candles. The timing would work out perfectly.

I enjoyed my shower and put on a sexy little black dress. I turned on the TV and sat back all cool and fresh like I had been waiting. I decided to talk to the girls while I waited. They reported that everything was fine, and they couldn't wait to get to New York. Naturally, I lied about how I'd only had time for work, and they were lucky they weren't here yet. We said our can't-wait-to-see-yous and hung up.

I looked quickly to make sure I hadn't missed a call from Mike. I hadn't. I thought about calling him. Then I had a better idea. *I'll go to bed and act like I am fast asleep when he gets here. Then he will take me in his strong arms and ...* My daydream continued as I drifted off to sleep.

***

I awoke to the sound of thunder. I quickly realized that Mike was not next to me. I glanced outside to see the storm I suspected. Mike's truck was not in the parking lot. I looked quickly to the clock on the stove. It was late. Mike should have called. I hoped I hadn't slept through his call. I should've been close to getting over the jet lag. I dialed Mike's number. But there was no answer. I thought I must have missed his visit. I hoped he would forgive me. I called again, but still there was no answer. I was upset and felt irritated. Then my phone rang.

"Mike? I was just about asleep again. This jet lag thing has got me bad this time," I said. "Mike, I need—"

"Hey, babe, I am glad you are getting some sleep," he said, interrupting me. "One of the apartment buildings just burned down. I have been with the police, fire department, and insurance company all night. I will call you in the morning. Good night."

Wait! I thought. He didn't even ask how I was. I couldn't believe I'd fallen asleep waiting for him! I wished he knew that I could have had a date tonight with a cute state trooper, that I didn't have to wait for his lame excuse. I calmed myself and tried to give him the benefit of the doubt since he was in crisis mode with the tragedy that had just taken place.

Here I was, six thousand miles away from everything I knew. Hawaii was not just my home; it was a way of life. And I was willing to give it up every so often to be with him. But it seemed he always had something else more important going on. When would I be more important? When would I come first? Then I remembered the "business first" rule. I still thought a phone call sooner would've been nice. I decided I would call him a bit later to see if he was okay.

My call went directly to the annoying lady telling me the person I had called was not available at the moment and suggesting, "Please try your call again later."

"What?" I shouted out loud. "He has turned off his friggin' phone for the evening!" He hadn't even bothered to call and let me know that everything was okay. I felt totally used at that point. Was I that sixteen-year-old good girl who got dumped when there was something better to be had?

How could he? I thought. He knew I was basically here for him. Business sucked, and there was nothing I could do here that I couldn't do from home. What the heck? I threw myself down on the floor. I felt all the pain of those awful teenage years coming back.

Was this what a broken heart felt like? God, I thought I might not make it until morning. I wished I wouldn't. Nothing else mattered right then. I wanted to feel his hands on my body, his lips on my lips, him inside of me.

"Oh my god!" I shouted out loud. I was crazed, with tears streaming down my face. *Let it all out, Tia*, I told myself, like I told my girls when they had a problem. *Just let it out. You'll feel better in the morning.* I sobbed, my body writhing. My heart was breaking, and oh god, it hurt so bad. As I lay there on the bedroom floor, uncontrollably sobbing, I made plans to leave and never look back. I told myself that in the morning I would *not* feel better. I vowed I would try to be more understanding of broken hearts as they happened in my household. But for that night, I just wanted to sob and feel bad for myself. The man I loved was a thoughtless jerk!

CHAPTER 13

My Turn to Call the Shots

Waking up from a night of crying was like waking up the day after running a marathon, or at least that was what I would've guessed, given that I had never run a marathon. This relationship felt like a marathon, though, and I was tackling Heartbreak Hill. I had no crowd cheering to get me over it, but at least I had music. No love songs on my iPod! Girl-power songs only, like "I Am Woman, Hear Me Roar." "Feel My Wrath" would've been a good song choice for that day. I smiled to myself. At least my sense of humor was intact.

I stumbled into the bathroom and gasped at the sight of my puffy eyes. I remembered I had kept some sample anti-aging packets from a vendor. I would've tried anything. I turned the shower nozzle to hot and let it run while I got my coffee. I tried not to look at my phone, but it was pulling me like a magnet—a Mike magnet. No surprise, it was already nine thirty, and he hadn't called.

I wondered what Mike would say if I just packed it all in and gave it up. At this point all I was doing was throwing money away for an excuse to be with him, and he was doing the same thing.

Of course, we hadn't gone over the numbers in detail this trip. Heck, we hadn't even seen each other for more than five minutes. Maybe he was hoping I would get sick of it all and leave. Maybe he was tired of losing money and didn't want to say anything. But I couldn't back out, not yet. I spoke to myself in the mirror. "You are not running away, Tia. Face this relationship and deal with it like it is business. Get the answers you so desperately need. Take the good and bad and roll with it. Enough! Stand up for your heart."

I saw Mike's eyes in the mirror, looking back at me, telling me it was okay to be mad at him. God, I loved that man. He was even guiding me through my heartbreak over him. Somehow Mr. Boss had become everything to me. Maybe I didn't want to talk about us because I was scared of how it might end up. If I left with no reason to come back, would he even care, or would he be relieved?

My ringing phone brought me back to reality and the cold New York morning.

"Hi, Mom," my girls sang in unison.

"Morning, girlies. You are up either super early or super late," I said.

"Well ..." Zoe said.

Sarah quickly interrupted. "Zoe can't sleep, so she thinks everyone should be up with her."

"Oh, be quiet, Sarah. Mom, I am so excited to come to New York and of course see you. Are you that busy?" Zoe asked.

"Oh, yes. Really busy and waiting for my girlies to get here," I told them. What I really wanted to say was "Men suck, and I really need some girl time, like a hike or a Lifetime movie day." Twenty-four hours had changed a lot. Yesterday, I was so in love and considered this man to be everything. Today I was puffy-eyed and almost ready to close the business that had kept me coming here to see him. I was also ready to swear off men for another ten years.

"Do you still have your ticket confirmations, or should I send them again so you can print your boarding passes?' I asked, already knowing Zoe would have everything organized.

"Got it, Mom," Zoe chimed in, "and I will even do Sarah's for her, if she is nice." I could tell they were giggling and having fun with each other.

"Well, try to get some sleep. I have got to get to work. I love you so much, girls."

"We love you too, Mom," they said loudly.

I hung up the phone and was left to face the day alone.

My morning routine was a little slower than normal as I struggled to keep focused on the tasks at hand. My brain kept wandering into the inevitable conversation. What would I say? What would he say? How would he react? I kept playing scenarios out in my mind and talking to myself in the mirror as I prepped to face my day. After one final glance in the full-length mirror, off I went.

As I reached for the door handle, I was startled by a loud knock. I swung the door open and heard that familiar voice. "Were you waiting at the door for me?" Mr. Boss smiled.

"You are kidding, right? As a matter of fact, I'm off to the spa to start the selling process. I will give it one month, and if it doesn't sell, I will close it down and get out of here," I said as I pushed past him.

His smile quickly faded. "Hey, wait! What are you talking about? Aren't we going to talk about this first?" He calmly walked alongside me. "You just got here. Tia, now you have a place, the girls are coming, and you can finally really dig into the business," he stated matter-of-factly.

"To be honest, I'm making decisions with the spa that I wouldn't otherwise make if it weren't for you. I know you have the same feelings and thoughts," I said.

"Is that so? Go on, tell me more," he said and waited.

"I'm not sure where to start—or end for that matter. I want out, Mike! This is not working for me, sitting around, waiting for you to give me five minutes of your time … you can't even pick up the phone to say hello … or that you miss me." I started to cry.

He grabbed my hand and gently led me back inside. "Let's start with I miss you," he said.

"It's a bit late for that," I said, pulling away from him.

"Tia, I haven't had you in months, and here you are standing in front of me, so beautiful I just want to feel you. I need you right now."

"Oh, so after three days you suddenly need me right now? What happened with the other days?" I blurted out. I was full of hurt and anger.

He softly ran his hand down my arm, folded his hand into mine, and gently pulled me toward him.

My head was spinning, and I said, "What, do you think you can come in here and just take me? After last night, after the last *two* nights, are you out of your mind?" I wanted him so badly, but I refused to give in. *Say no, Tia*, I told myself. *Yes, you need him too, but he broke your heart last night, and it needs to heal. Does giving him your body even make sense? You need to stay strong!*

"Sorry, Mike. Not this time. It's not that easy. I am going down to the spa to collect all the books, and I will come to your office, and we will make a business decision based on the numbers I have to show you," I explained.

"Tia, I know what the numbers are, and no, they aren't that good. But it is difficult to maintain being absent from the business 50 percent of the time." He was being sarcastic.

"Oh, so I am to blame? Maybe if I hadn't been waiting around for you all the time, my head would have been more in order when I was here."

"Tia, I've been doing my part, and Clare follows up every day."

"What? Do you have her checking up on me?" I asked.

"No, don't be silly. She is my assistant, and that's what assistants do."

"When you called her the other night, did you know that we were having dinner together?" I asked accusingly.

He shook his head. "No, she didn't tell me that."

"Then why did she have to go outside to talk to you, and not in front of me?" I sounded like the jealous woman I was becoming.

"She handles a lot of personal things for me, and that night I needed her to let me know certain information. I didn't want her around anyone. I didn't know she was with you. Please understand." He was beginning to plead, and I liked that.

"Why haven't you been around for me?" I demanded.

"I told you there was a fire, and I'm really busy with all the properties. I thought we had agreed that business comes first."

I was getting so tired of hearing that line. I just rolled my eyes. "Yes, we did, but we also talked about having some kind of balance when we're together. I travel six thousand miles every time to see you. Months ago, I would have sold the business, and now my life seems to revolve around you," I said, sobbing.

"Tia, I love you. There are just some things that you don't understand. I planned on telling you everything after the girls went back. I wanted to see if they like the place and how we can have some kind of future together ..."

Seeing sadness in those big, brown eyes was too much for me. "Oh, shut up, Mike, and kiss me! Tell me everything later. Let's sell or close the spa and work out our lives, but for now I have needs that I want fulfilled," I told him, and then I devoured him with my lips. He immediately responded. We savagely kissed one another and soon found ourselves in the bedroom, with clothes flying. Naked, we rolled around on the bed, hungry with love and lust. I didn't know what had come over me, but this time I wanted to take control.

He gasped in response to one small bite I placed on his inner thigh.

"Oh, sorry ... too hard, sweetheart?" I purred.

"Yeah, a little," he agreed, looking a trite shocked.

"Deal with it," I told him.

I felt a rush of certainty in every move I was making. It seemed that woman inside of me with all the confidence had shown up. I was getting used to her making herself known more often those days, but never during lovemaking. *This should be interesting*, I thought.

He moaned and groaned. I thought I could hear a smile on those lips that I intended to devour in a few moments.

"Baby, I have missed you," I told him fiercely. "You just relax, and I am going to do all those things I have been fantasizing about. It may take a while. You okay with that?"

"I'm good, baby. I am just going to let you take control," he whispered.

I hadn't waited for his reply. I was already devouring his hardness. Oh god, had I missed this jewel in my mouth. I could tell by the way his body reacted that this was almost torturous for him.

I heard him moan. "Oh god, baby, that's my girl. Holy shit, have you been practicing?" he asked.

I never thought this would become such a turn-on for me. I was experiencing the entire realm of senses—sight, sound, touch, taste, and smell! I felt it all, and it was incredible. I heard him moan and realized at that moment I was in complete control. That made me even more passionate than before, and I let my emotions, body, and nature take control.

"Baby, I want you now," he said.

Of course, I wanted him inside of me, but I was enjoying myself right where I was. "Okay, okay, it's time," I finally said, sliding up underneath him.

"No, on your tummy," he instructed.

This was something new, and I gladly did as I was told.

"Your man is going to take you from behind," he stated. Quickly, he added, "Is that okay?"

In an instant I was on all fours, and he was taking me as promised. As he expertly placed his hands on my hips to enter me, I felt so desired and so feminine, letting go of the control I'd held a moment ago.

"Take me, baby," I moaned. Climaxing before I could even give notice, I felt him going too.

"On your back," he said quickly.

He entered me again, and we started the rhythm of our usual lovemaking.

"God, I missed you, babe," I whispered between kisses.

"I missed you too. Do know how much I love you?" he asked gently, looking into my eyes.

"Yes, I do. I just get a little crazy," I said, putting my face to his.

><·<>·O·<>·<

We lay there for a moment, exhausted and enjoying the silence. "What are you thinking?" he said after a few minutes.

"Truth?"

"Nothing but the truth."

"I'm thinking about how much I love you, how this moment in time was meant to be."

"Hmm," he groaned. He broke the silence again to ask, "Can I get a back rub?"

"Of course, I would love to release some stress while we talk," I said with enthusiasm.

I loved rubbing Mike's back. Feeling the tense muscles beneath my hands and being able to work the tension out was very satisfying and intimate for me. There was a flow to our conversations during these back rubs too. It was easy, almost like pillow talk. Our conversation this time turned to the spa. We both realized the spa had problems. I needed to either sell the entire business or close it down. It wouldn't work with an absentee owner. We considered most options, but they were all unrealistic. We were both losing money and couldn't keep this up just for the sake of our relationship.

We turned our attention toward the girls and their arrival in the next few days. I reminded him they had no clue about us. I thought that was for the best, and he agreed, at least until we figured out what was going to happen with us. I did suggest that he try to get to know them better.

"I must take a shower," I said, and he agreed loudly.

"What?" I said, giggling. "Am I that stinky?"

"Oh yes," he said, rolling me over. "You are so stinky, but it is a good stinky," he laughed. "When exactly are the girls getting in?"

"Four days," I said, half-smiling, half-grimacing. I was so excited to see them, but I was also feeling a little unsure. He could tell and leaned in for a kiss.

"It'll all be okay. Trust me, Tia," he said reassuringly.

I kissed those wonderful lips of his and looked into his honorable eyes.

CHAPTER 14

Back to Business

Days went by quickly, with work and play often intermingling as the girls' arrival approached. Mr. Boss had his business-first rule, which I understood. I had my kids-first and business-second rule, which would put Mike third. We had not crossed that bridge, but we soon would.

I was at the spa when my phone rang. It was Mike. "Annie, I need to answer this call, but stay here. We aren't finished."

I answered my phone. "Hey, can I call you right back? I am in a meeting," I explained.

"Yes, of course." He hung up without saying good-bye. At that moment I loved the "business comes first" rule. Maybe that was a little selfish. I put my phone away and continued my discussion with Annie.

"After next week we will also start scaling back anyone who doesn't have a full schedule. I know it doesn't seem right, but business is business, and we need to keep as much revenue as we can coming in until we sell ... or, unfortunately, close," I said sadly.

"I think your idea of giving 'How to Own Your Own Spa' presentations is great. I have sent out the invitations to our customer base," Annie said proudly. "And already we are getting a good response."

"That makes me happy. I only hope that we can find a buyer because the place is amazing, and the atmosphere that you have helped to create is relaxing," I said, smiling. "Annie, I don't want the employees to know that we are being forced to take steps to close. I would rather they think that I'm selling possible franchise opportunities. So we will tell them in the last two weeks and do what we need to do then. Any questions?"

"No, I have a feeling that it will all work out, and we will find a buyer," she said, confidently looking back at me.

I was reminded of just how far she had come since I hired her. I had promised Annie other work if the spa closed. If the spa sold, I promised I would work out an agreement with the new owner for her continued work. She was a good, honest employee. I smiled at her as I passed through the lobby on my way to the door.

That night was a perfect night. I had no more worries about where the business was headed, and my girls would be there in a few days. I smiled and headed to the gym to lose myself in music and pain.

><+>+O+<+><

Sweaty and totally exhausted, I wondered why I had run to the gym. The sun had set, and the stars were starting to appear in the early evening sky. On my way back home I decided to take a shortcut through a wetland-like area. I saw blinking lights and wondered what they were. I soon realized they were fireflies. I remembered my mom telling me about them when I was a kid. She had grown up in Florida and had fond memories of chasing them at night.

I sat down and got lost in the moment. An hour had gone by when I heard my phone ring. By then it was completely dark.

"I thought you were going to call me right back?" Mike said.

"Oh my goodness, Mike, I totally forgot. I am so sorry. I got busy with Annie, and then I went to the gym and—"

"It's okay," he said. "I am just busting your chops. I got busy too. What are you doing?"

"Well, I have to tell you, I am watching fireflies, and they are so beautiful," I said with enthusiasm.

"Fireflies?" he said. "Where are you?"

"I was walking home from the gym and cut across that little road. You know the one right behind that little shopping plaza?"

"What? What are you doing there in the dark? I'm coming to get you now! I'll be there in two minutes." I could hear the panic in his voice.

That made me nervous, and I started to think about where I was. I was in New York. I hunkered down, no longer enjoying my little friends. Then every little noise frightened me. My fears left me as Mr. Boss's truck pulled up.

"Hey," I said, opening the passenger door.

"Hey, yourself. Don't be coming out here in the dark. You need to be careful. This isn't Maui," he stated sternly.

"Okay, but I have you to watch out for me," I joked, trying to ease the tension.

"I'm serious, Tia. You need to let the girls know this as well when they get here. This is not a place to be at night." He pulled me close and hugged me.

I was taking in this new side of Mr. Boss. "You are concerned for your woman's safety?" I teased.

"Tia, I am serious," he growled.

"I know, I know," I said. "Did you see the fireflies?"

"No, I just want to get you home," he said grumpily.

I suddenly remembered that I was in my gym clothes and sweaty, with my hair up. I was a mess! "I need a shower when we get home," I said, hoping he would get the hint that I knew I looked bad. He was beautifully dressed in a suit and tie.

"Yeah, I see that. And I smell that," he laughed.

"Oh, you are too funny. At least I did a full workout. Did you?" I asked, pushing him in fun.

"Tia, I want to take you out to dinner tonight. I have something important to talk about," Mike said seriously.

"I would like that very much."

Once we arrived at the apartment, I ran straight to the shower. "I'll be right out. Just going to rinse," I said, laughing out loud.

"Take your time," he insisted, laughing. "Can I pour you some wine?"

"Yes, please. I won't be long."

Fifteen minutes later, I was ready, with hair and makeup done. I put on a beautiful, sexy red dress, off the shoulders. Feeling amazing, I walked out of the bedroom with a big smile.

"Well, hello," he stammered.

Mr. Boss was looking for words, so I knew I must look good. I was more confident than ever, and the lighting was perfectly flattering. He took my hand and kissed my mouth.

"Let's go," he said. "I have plans for you later. This will give me a chance to sit across from you and take you all in—you are beautiful, Tia!"

✦ ┼ ✦❯ ❖ ❬✦ ┼ ❖

As we were seated at the restaurant, I noticed a few people looking at us. Wouldn't it have been wonderful to know they were looking at what a striking couple we made? Instead, I was concerned about whether he knew anyone here, or more importantly, whether his daughter knew anyone who would take photos and send to her. That wasn't the way we wanted her to find out. Thank goodness I didn't have those worries with my daughters. I thought about how we would hide our relationship if he were to come to Maui. For a moment, I wondered whether we should have told everyone early on. I knew, though, that this would have been impossible between his legal issues with his soon-to-be ex-wife and my not wanting to drag my children into something that might not even last.

The waiter broke into my thoughts. "And for you, ma'am?"

"Oh yes, I would like to have water with no ice for now, please." As the waiter left, I looked around at the wood and rock decor. "This restaurant is beautiful, Mike," I said.

We just didn't have this kind of decor on Maui. All the high-end restaurants were open-air. They were mainly made of marble and slate for easy upkeep with our weather. Of course, they were updated every few years for the tourists, and it was all very modern.

"I love this old style, and the wood brings such warmth to the atmosphere." I smiled while looking around. "Throw in the rock fireplace as the center focal point in the room, and you have romance."

"Yes, I love the wood too. I think you make this room romantic, though, not the fireplace." He smiled back at me.

I have never had dinner with someone where I felt like we were the only people in the room. Another first, I thought.

"Tia, I want to talk to you seriously tonight. As much as I love the dinner conversation and the romance of this place, I feel that I need to explain some personal things that are going on in my life. I hope you understand and remember the commonality we seem to share—that is, not letting people get too close."

"I understand, Mike, and I want to have this conversation with you because I am becoming a little paranoid when it comes to your lack of availability."

"My lack of communicating my whereabouts comes from two reasons. First, I'm a very private person, and the other reason, quite frankly, is my fear of being disappointed. I often think it's less of a risk to go it alone," Mike explained. He reached out to touch my hand. I gave him my hand graciously, and he continued.

"I have found someone I want to let in, someone I need to let in," he said, smiling warmly.

"Mike, I am slowly learning too. We are breaking into a new way of communicating, which I have never had before."

"I know, Tia. As we go forward, we must open ourselves up, sharing difficult personal tragedies and emotional issues ..." He trailed off as the waiter walked up and asked if we would like to order.

Darn, he'd had a good speech going there. I wanted him to keep speaking from his heart. At the same time I felt a little concerned. Was he going to tell me that we needed to cool things down for a little while until the girls were older and his issues were settled?

"What would you like, Tia?"

"I would like for you to decide and surprise me."

As soon as I said that, the waiter jumped in and told Mike what they were offering "just for two." All I could do was wish for the waiter to leave. I couldn't stand the suspense. My heart was hanging on the line.

Mike listened attentively to the waiter and began to make his selections for the food and the wine that would complement the dish. I quickly excused myself to use the restroom.

"Sure, sweetheart, take your time. I've got it!" He stood as I got up to leave.

The trip to the bathroom was my excuse to gain some confidence back. I looked deep into my own eyes in the mirror and started talking to the image staring back at me. "Tia, it's okay to reassure yourself. Whatever he has to say, you'll deal with it like business. Take the emotion out of it, girlfriend! Be strong. Be the Tia you feel safe as. If he wants to end it, you can retreat back behind that lovely wall you have been working on for so many years."

I ran my hands through my blonde hair. I did like the way I looked that night. I took a deep breath and concentrated on the task at hand. I looked forward to hearing what he had to say, and who knew? He might surprise me.

"Welcome back," he said, standing up for me to sit down. "I ordered us some white wine, and we are having the duck, but first here is your glass. I want to make a toast before I continue on with my serious talk." He raised his glass and said, "To the most beautiful woman in the world."

We clinked our glasses together, and before taking a sip, I said, "Well, thank you, kind sir. I would love to drink to that." I was feeling even more confident.

"As I was saying, or rambling, I guess ... bear with me, as this subject is very difficult for me to talk about, but I do know it is time." Mike lowered his eyes for a few seconds.

I took a deep breath and prepared for the worst. However, I had enough compassion for this man to realize this was very difficult, and I reached out to grab his hand. "It's okay, Mike. I have all night." I was really thinking, *Get this over with so I can get on with a long night of sobbing.*

"Tia, I know there are a lot of times I cannot get to the phone when you call and ... sometimes I'm so exhausted that I literally pass out when I get home," he said. He stopped and seemed to be gathering his thoughts. "You know my mother has been ill. What you don't know is that she has needed constant care for the last few years. It breaks my heart to see her suffering. She has had a rough life, and the ending for her is not pleasant either." I saw the tears welling up in his soulful eyes.

"I witnessed the physical abuse my father placed upon my mother. I felt as helpless then as I do now."

I held his hand even tighter.

"Excuse me," he said as he rolled his eyes up as if to get rid of the tears before they actually fell down his face. "We have moved her into a home for better care. I have been doing everything I can, burning the candle at both ends. Some nights my brother can't get down to take care of her, and I cover for him. That is when I appear mysterious and don't let you know. She needs to know we are still here and care deeply for her. I want her to feel as much love as possible. She has really gone downhill the last couple of weeks, and now it's not a matter of checking in on her and getting her to bed; it's staying with her most of the night so she doesn't get scared or get up and hurt herself."

"Mike, what stopped you from telling me? Did you think I wouldn't understand?" I asked, concerned.

"I didn't want to burden you. Our relationship was new, and I know you have enough to worry about." He smiled and kissed my hand.

I was so relieved. I had imagined all kinds of things, including that his wife had come back into the picture, but now I knew the truth. This showed me that it was time to start trusting this man. "What is her condition today? Babe, I want to know and be there for you."

"She needs dialysis, but they can't do it because her heart only functions at 20 percent. She is in a lot of pain and takes a load of medications. It is sad for me when I see her, knowing that her time is limited, but what upsets me the most is that she is not the same mom I had five years ago."

"Mike, this is hard on you, but we all have to go sometime, and you are doing all you can for her. Please don't be so hard on yourself," I said, bursting with love for this man.

"When I leave her, sometimes I just want to curl up in a ball and cry myself to sleep. I can't call you when I'm with her, and afterward it seems like I would be a downer to be with. There is nothing I want to do but feel sorry for myself. Nobody wants to be around someone like that," he reluctantly told me and took another sip of wine.

"Don't assume things, Mike. I would always be there for you, and now that I understand, I won't be threatening to leave you every other trip." I tried a little laugh, and he did crack a smile.

"Tia, seeing her makes me worry about my own heart. I have had two open-heart surgeries in the last fifteen years."

"What? You never told me this," I said, shocked.

"Yes, that is not a good record, and yes, medicine is light-years from where it was when she started having heart problems. But just knowing I have that condition, sometimes I feel I shouldn't burden another person with what I could go through. I already have to put my daughter through it. Do I knowingly want to put you or your girls through it?" Mike looked at me with genuine concern, and I totally understood.

"Oh my god," I said, looking into those wonderful eyes. "I don't know what to say. 'I am so sorry' sounds so cliché, but necessary, I guess. I can't begin to know what you are going through. I can only imagine the mental and emotional burden. But I will say, instead of not letting me in and trying to protect me from the unknown, you should let that be my choice." I smiled. "Don't you think?" I squeezed his hand.

Our dinner arrived, and I had to admit that the duck was delicious. We decided not to discuss his mom over dinner, and instead we talked about his daughter, his stepson in Colorado, my girls, his business, and my businesses in New York and in Hawaii. In doing so, we both had the realization that our responsibilities were real and couldn't be taken lightly. I began to think our life together would need to take a backseat. I could tell he was feeling the same.

"With all these things I have on my mind night and day," he said, "running the business is taking a toll on my time and me. I hope this explains my absence and not paying you the attention you deserve." He smiled and squeezed my hand as if to say he was finished talking.

"I will be here for you, Mike. Whatever craziness is thrown our way, and for however long, is not for us to decide."

He held my hand to his face and pressed it against his cheek. "I love you, Tia Malone," he whispered.

Mike took care of the check, and we left. Getting into the car, we both agreed it was time to forget all this seriousness and have some "us" time.

It had been a wonderful, enlightening evening, and I felt closer than ever to Mike as we returned to the apartment. I had accepted the way things were for us because now I knew what our relationship was burdened with. Tonight six thousand miles seemed the least of our troubles.

I walked into the apartment beside him, and the lighting was perfectly flattering. I was freshly shaved and perfumed everywhere. I smiled to myself, for I had just the thing to change the mood that hung over us. *Time to use my handbook on how to talk dirty to your man*, I decided.

I took hold of his hand and began to walk toward the bedroom, and then instantly, I changed my mind. I saw the confused look on his face when I dropped his hand and forced him down on to the couch.

"Why are you still dressed?" I questioned sternly.

"I don't know, but I can change that right now," he said as he started ripping off his clothing. He sat back down in nothing but what God gave him, and I must say, God had been very generous.

"Hmm," I groaned as I took hold of his erect manhood. He was a beautiful man. I fondled him with my hand as I began kissing his neck. I trailed my tongue down his body until I reached the treasure I was holding, all the while telling him how I couldn't wait to have him.

"The way you're thrusting lets me know you want it, baby. I love that," he panted.

"You want to have your girl? You want me, baby? You just sit back and let me take you. God, have I missed you in my mouth. I am so wet, baby. I can hardly wait to have you take me."

I took him in my mouth and heard him groan louder than ever. I smiled to myself as I took him in. It seemed the dirty-talk book worked. I just had to get better and better.

"Holy shit. Oh god, baby, I can't wait. I have to have you now," he begged.

I wanted to make him wait and give him a little more taste of my dirty talk, but I couldn't wait either. I stood up and was headed to the bedroom when I felt his hands on my waist, stopping me in an instant. He pulled me down to the floor and took me right there.

Oh my god, the lighting, the low noise, the dirty talk. I didn't know what it was, but the climaxes were stronger. Oh my god, this was insane. How could sex be so good on the living room floor? Did I feel the hard floor beneath me? No. Did I feel the carpet giving me rug burns? No. I just felt Mr. Boss loving me, fucking me, and loving me some more. Yes, there was a difference, but it was great. It was fantastic. There were no words! I was definitely his lioness, willing, whenever, wherever. I was his for as long as we could have each other.

We lay quietly together on the floor as he stroked my hair, and our heavy breathing subsided. No words were necessary, and we were totally satisfied. Minutes later, he broke the silence.

"When are the girls arriving?"

I counted down in my head. "Um, two days."

"Do you miss them?" he asked.

I thought that was a strange question. "Of course. I always do. I am concerned about us when they get here, though."

"Why?" he asked.

"I don't want them to know about us until we know if we have a future."

"I agree, and I respect that. I will be, as always, your devoted business partner," he laughed. "Now, missy, it is time for us to get some sleep."

"Oh, Mike. You are going to sleep with me all night?" I said excitedly. "Let me use the bathroom, and I'll see you in bed!" I rushed off to the bathroom, and as I closed the door, I heard the all-too-familiar sound of his ringtone. I waited to listen before I closed the door.

"Hello? Who's this?" he asked under his breath. "Shit! Are you sure? I'll be right there."

I closed the bathroom door and waited for him to tell me that he had to go.

T. MALONE

⊶≕ CHAPTER 15 ≓⊷

My Girlies Arrive

When I awoke the next day, it was a lovely morning, and I had slept well. I was over my jet lag and sleeping very well after all the extra exercise Mr. Boss and I were getting!

The girls were arriving the next day, and I was so not ready. I had some major scheduling and meetings to get to. Plus, I hadn't really gotten to the grocery store, and I knew the girls would want food.

I promised myself an emotion-free day. I had to learn to accept my relationship with Mike just the way it was. I had learned how to shut off emotions when it came to business, and now I must learn to make decisions that were best for the business. I wouldn't let personal feelings get in the way.

I heard the familiar ringtone and picked up my phone. "Hey, sexy," I said.

"Hey, yourself, and thanks for understanding last night." Mike sounded relieved.

"How is your mom today?" I asked.

"Good, babe! Good! What time can you have coffee with me, and I'll tell you all about it?" Mike suggested.

"Oh my gosh, Mike, I am so busy this morning with the girls arriving. I can't. Can we make it another morning this week? The girls will be sleeping in, I can guarantee it," I laughed.

"Yeah, okay."

I could hear the disappointment in his voice. I knew he had reached out to me regarding his mom. Shoot! *Bad timing*, I thought.

"I will talk to you later," he said. "Go get on with your busy day. I love you."

"I love you too, babe," I said.

As I went about my day, I realized something had changed in me. My whole life, I had been putting others first. Being the youngest child in our family hadn't allowed me to voice my opinion at a young age. I had been told as a little girl to keep my mouth shut for the sake of others' feelings or to keep the peace, and that was what I did.

It was time I started standing up for myself all the time. If that meant my relationship with Mr. Boss taking a backseat, he would need to understand I couldn't always be there for him without reservation, like I had been. He needed to understand that he was not the only one who had responsibilities. I must put my priorities first, just as he was doing.

I told myself that there were plenty of Mr. Bosses out there, and I certainly didn't need a man in my busy life to cramp my style. But I knew I was selling myself a load of crap. Deep down, I hoped we would make it. I was just glad at this point that I hadn't brought my girls into this relationship. I headed out the door with my newfound bravado.

As I entered the spa a few minutes later, my phone rang. "Hello, girlies. Are you on Oahu yet?" I waved hello to Annie. By the grim look on her face, I could tell she was going over budgets, and it wasn't good.

"Yes!" they squeaked in unison.

"We board our next flight in two hours and twelve minutes," Zoe stated.

"Okay, sounds like you're covered. Do you have enough snacks for the flight? It's a long one, you know, and this time of year, it's an additional forty-five minutes. Have you got the flight cards I left for you if you want more food, drinks, or blankets on the plane?" I asked, like the typical mother.

"Yes, Mom," answered Sarah. "Zoe just went to get another water. You scared her with the additional flying time comment."

"Why don't you guys go get some lunch, do some yoga stretches, and give me a call when you're boarding so I can start worrying?" I smiled. I knew she was smiling too.

"Okay, Mom. Love you. Bye."

"Bye, Sarah." I hung up and went to tend to that look Annie had on her face. "Okay, Annie, let me have it," I said.

"Well, Tia. With the schedule change and the cut in hours for the therapists who are not pulling their weight, I see better numbers for the bottom line. But not as good as I know you'd hoped. However, I think they are good enough to entice a buyer," she said.

"Well, it certainly looks from a glance like it could happen. I'm going to be in the office. I have some other paperwork to do. Let's meet later today on this; I have some ideas. As usual, this is confidential, Annie," I reminded her seriously. "Oh, can you schedule the girls for a wrap and short massage the day after tomorrow? I want to get them in for their jet lag treatment ... I can't handle the crabbiness this trip, that's for sure."

She smiled back. "Sure thing, Tia. Is that with the usual therapists?"

"Hmm, yes," I said, nodding my head, as I walked toward the office.

>─┼◆◆─○─◆┼─<

I scanned the paperwork one more time and decided that I should call Mike to get his opinion on the selling price and question him on what he could do to help the new owner as far as the lease was concerned. This could be a turning point. Of course, he was not answering. I called his office, and Clare answered with her usual charm.

"Well, good morning, darling," I said, chuckling.

"Hey, Tia! Are the girls here?" she asked.

"Tomorrow. Have you seen Mike today? I have to talk to him; it's important, and he's not answering his phone."

"As per the normal. I haven't seen him yet, but I know he has a closing at the new development this afternoon. If you want, I can call the real estate office and leave word for him to call you ASAP if he hasn't talked to you before," she offered.

I wondered what she would say if she knew about us. The office definitely would be buzzing.

"That will be great, Clare. Thanks."

"Don't forget to bring the girls by," she said before hanging up.

Clare was one of those people who made me wonder whether she liked me for me or for information she could get out of me. I was beginning to question her motives and just what role she thought she played with Mike. Maybe I was feeling jealous. I scolded myself mid-thought. "Cut it out, Tia," I said aloud. I tried Mike's cell again.

Where was he? What was he doing? Couldn't he at least pick up and say, 'I'll call right back'? I knew he was probably in a meeting. But this was important, and we needed to decide on the selling price that day. The girls were coming in the next day, and this couldn't wait. I had to know what I would say once inquiries started coming to me on the purchase price and lease conditions. I decided to use the emergency call code Mike and I had put in place. If either of us needed the other immediately, we would call once, hang up, and within thirty seconds call right back, alerting the other it was an emergency. I wasn't sure this was that kind of emergency, but I did need to talk to him immediately. If he had voice mail or text messaging, this would not be an issue! I called, hung up, and immediately dialed again.

Then I waited to see if he remembered the pact. What if he was with his mom? Oh, goodness, I hoped not. It was too late. This was business. I consoled myself. My phone rang, and I smiled. Yes, it was Mr. Boss.

"Hey," I said.

"Hey, what's up? Everything okay?" I could hear concern in his voice.

"Well, yes. But I need to talk to you. The ads for the sale of the spa have gone out. I need to talk to you regarding the asking price, but more importantly, what you want as far as the rent and lease terms, as you know that will make a big difference to the buyer. We should have talked about this before. I have some ideas, and Annie and I are still planning a sales presentation next week. We have invited our client base, and the topic will be how to own your own spa. We can let them think that I'm looking to franchise, and it just may be a way to attract some buyers. What do you think?" I asked.

"Sounds like you have a good plan. I will need to get right back to you. I'm afraid I can't think right now," he answered.

"Mike, the girls will be here tomorrow, and I need to move on this today!" I told him anxiously. "Are you available this afternoon? I know you have a closing. Can you meet me before that?"

"Oh shit, I forgot about the closing. No ... Tia, I'm at the hospital with my mom. I had to bring her in last night after I left you. I was going to explain everything over coffee. She has taken a turn for the worse."

"Oh god, Mike, what happened?" I said. I felt terrible for having doubted him again and for placing all those stereotypes about men on him. It seemed like I had implemented the emergency phone call system when I had no real emergency!

"More complications, I'm afraid, but she is almost ninety. I'll probably get someone else to do the closing. My brother is coming to the hospital a little later. I am just waiting to talk to her doctor. Then I can stop by. Is that all right?"

"Uh, yeah, whatever. I'll be here all day. I'm sorry."

I felt lame. As I started to prepare the paperwork for our meeting, I began to feel mistrusting of the situation again. It had happened too many times before. I knew his mom was sick, but the rest of his world ceased to exist, or at least that was how it seemed to me. Maybe next it would be his daughter or his stepson. I stopped my thoughts; they were very selfish.

>—+—+>—0—<+—+—<

"Aloha," I said, trying not to sound upset as I answered the phone.

"Hey, Mom, we are getting on the plane," said Sarah.

I was so glad I had the girls' arrival to look forward to. I wondered sometimes what life would hold when they had their own families and I didn't have them to look forward to every day. But today wasn't that day.

"It's time for you to start worrying," Sarah said, breaking my train of thought.

"Okay, starting now. Call as soon as you land. Then I can take a break until you board your next flight here, 'okay?"

"You got it," said Sarah.

"Love you!" both girls sang into the phone.

"I love you too, girlies. Have a great flight, and don't fight." Ha, there was that poet I knew I was. I smiled and hung up, just in time to hear Annie directing Mike to my office.

I quickly took down my hair and took my glasses off. I put on lip gloss, sprayed my body spray in the air, and barely got a stick of gum in my mouth before he entered. *Whew!*

"Hey," I said, smiling, as I stood to greet him.

"Hey," he said, looking tired and broken. I had never seen him look so slumped over before. I had almost forgotten the tragedy he was facing.

I came out from behind the desk and gave him a much-needed hug. "How is your mom? Any improvement?" I asked.

"She's better. Probably can go home tomorrow. I guess I need to face the fact that my mother is dying," he said, without letting go of me.

"I'm so sorry, Mike. I wish I could do something."

"That's life," he grumbled. "So what do we have going here, Miss Tia?" he asked as if he wanted to have a change in his day.

"Well, take a look at these numbers since we changed the schedule, or as Annie puts it, since the dead weight was taken away. With the drop in payroll and the increase in new clients from the better therapists, we are seeing a good shift. We have a viable reason to ask a buyer for a substantial amount for an ongoing established business. Here is the list of inventory; we have first-class equipment and decor. I know that depreciates, but it is all set up to operate for a few years without significant outlay. With these numbers, a new owner can definitely have a prosperous business. This will give me a chance to recoup some of my losses and let you have the appropriate rent coming in. I would hope that you could agree on a lesser figure and increase the rent over the next three months." As I concluded, I sat down and waited for a response.

"Oh, you do?" He smiled. "Most impressed!" He looked over the numbers I had worked on all morning. I couldn't tell from his expression what he was thinking. So I just waited. But I couldn't wait. I wanted to cut in, so I excused myself to the restroom.

As I opened the door to the office, he spoke. "What about us, Tia?" he asked, changing the subject completely. I think he had just then realized what had been there all along. I wouldn't be so readily available to visit New York.

Surprised, I thought quickly. This was business, and business came first; or was that just his business? I was pretty sure I had on my big-girl panties. *Here we go* was my last thought as my words escaped without warning. "What about us?" I fired back, not even thinking about his sadness any longer. Here she was, that woman who showed up in my defense.

"This is business, Mike. We need to finish what was started here without draining us both. You have a lot more pocket change to drain than I, but this is getting ridiculous. A new owner can be here and take this to a new level. I can't commit to this the way it needs. I should have seen that once my partner walked out. But I fell in love and wanted it to work. I can't let that cloud my judgment any longer." I waited for a response.

He smiled. "Well, Tia, I must say you are quite the businesswoman, aren't you? And when you're right, you're right! I'll do what's necessary on my end for the lease arrangements."

We discussed a fair asking price and other necessities that would be in the contract, contingent upon other reports. *That was easy*, I thought. He was right. I did know what I was doing. I was going to be okay.

"Now, what about us?" I said, using my tone to change the meaning of those words, letting him see I was feeling womanly, in every sense.

"Well, I can take you here," he said as he motioned toward my desk.

"Uh, I don't think so," I giggled, "but seriously?" I waited hopefully for his romantic gesture—a white horse, red rose type of response—but that was wishful thinking. That wasn't Mr. Boss, and that was okay, because most times it wasn't me either, but the woman he was pulling out of me was beginning to think more often about the romantic side of love.

"Well, what the hell is gonna get you back here to see me?" He startled me by going back to the previous conversation. I thought maybe the way my brain jumped back and forth was rubbing off on him. "We have both hung on to this business for a reason. Now what?" he asked. Now it was his turn to wait.

I looked down at my desk like the answers were in my notes somewhere. My mind was blank. I hadn't banked on having that conversation right then. *I started it*, I thought, *so I guess I'll finish it.*

"I can't bring my girls into a relationship when I don't know where it's headed, Mike—you know that. I do need a reason to come here. The more I fall in love with you, the more I need to see you, and the harder all this has become," I said apprehensively. "I lean to you for those answers. I put my work and girls on hold in the islands to come and see you. You need to come up with the answer for this to work. I have another year or so with my girls at home, so ..." I purposely let my voice trail off. "So if we find a buyer who takes on the business package, I may be able to come back, but that would only be a couple of times ..." I trailed off again.

"Let me sleep on it. I have so much on my brain right now, I can't even think straight. I do love you, and that I know." He looked into my eyes.

"I love you too, Mike." I looked back at him, proud of the conversations that had just taken place. I was proud that I had stood up for my business, for my girls, and finally for myself.

"What time do the girls get in?" he asked.

"Not till after midnight, but I have a ton to do, plus I have to get to the grocery store, or at least make a list for Annie to get to the store."

"Okay. Dinner?" he said, holding my hand.

"Yes, of course. What time? Where?"

"Let's go to Sansei. Seven sharp."

"Promise," I said.

"Promise," he said as he turned and walked out of my office.

God, I love that smile, I thought.

Pressing the intercom button on my office phone, I said, "Annie, I need that list of potential buyers, or should I say *guests* for the presentation."

Annie slipped in with the list within minutes, like she had already known what I was thinking.

"I saw Mike leave, and I knew you would be ready to get on this," she explained, putting the paperwork down on my desk.

"Thanks. By the way, are you very busy after work?"

"No, why?"

"I need a huge favor. I have not been to the market, and the girls will be here, and I … well, I desperately need food for them. Could you perhaps get my list done for me after work and drop it off at the apartment? I'll give you a free massage with your favorite therapist," I said with a laugh.

"Of course, Tia, but I'll pass on the massage. I planned on leaving late today anyway, and since you're here, I'll just go now to the market."

"You're a lifesaver, Annie. I'll call the manager and let her know you'll be stopping by so that she can let you into the apartment."

Annie left, and I quickly called the apartment manager before I forgot. I then proceeded to make twenty calls off the list of potential buyers. I was able to secure five meetings for the weekend. I planned to invite them to the presentation next week as well.

I implemented my marketing plan and then decided to finish up my sales presentation and graphs along with a few handouts for the group sales presentation that I had planned for Sunday. I knew that after dinner with Mike, we would have other things to do. I noticed the shadows on my desk and immediately looked at my watch.

Oh my god, dinner! It was already 7:05 p.m. Shoot, Mike was probably waiting for me. Crud! I knew at the very least I had to change my clothes. I tried to reassure myself with our mantra: "business comes first." Besides, he was always late. *I'll call him now*, I thought. He normally didn't even call, so my calling should make up for my lateness, I figured.

As I gathered my things and headed for the door, I dialed his number, thinking or hoping that some of my good habits were rubbing off on him because it definitely seemed some of his bad habits were rubbing off on me.

"Yes?" he said in his low voice.

"Hey, I'm sorry. I got into the whole sales plan, and time got away … I am headed to change now. Save me a seat, order me a glass of wine, and I'll be there before the server brings it, I promise!" I was babbling, and I knew I sounded guilty.

"It's okay, Tia." I could tell he was smiling.

God, how did he do it—not get upset? I thought about how upset I would be, although sometimes or most times I didn't show it, so maybe he just wasn't showing it. On the other hand, he was mindful that I was deep in work, so his calm attitude went along with his business-first rule. That did make me feel safe to dive into work and lose all track of time without feeling guilty. That was a great feeling. I made a mental note to be more understanding, at least in my own mind.

"I'll go one step further," he said. "Because I have to get back to my mom, I'll order your dinner. How's that?"

It was one of the few times I had heard a bit of uncertainty in his voice. Was he unsure of himself on this one, or was this about our conversation earlier? Whatever it was, I kind of liked him not knowing whether he was going to get what he wanted.

"How is she?" I asked, biting my lip.

"Oh, she's holding her own, for now. She's got three of us kids to check in on her, so she'll be okay. I'm just going numb. I guess it's the not knowing."

He sounded like he needed conversation of the feminine kind. I noted that and decided I would be just that at dinner. This was a side of me that had begun to feel natural, and I had begun to cherish rather than hide it.

"What do you want to eat, sweetheart?" he asked. "I know you love the lobster here since you don't get it at home. Well, at least you don't get it fresh." He was definitely right about that. "Have you had any yet this trip?"

"No, I have not. That would be great, babe. I'll be there soon. One more favor?"

"Yes?"

"Call your friends at the state troopers and tell them that a maroon Nissan will be hauling tail down Route 9 to meet her lover for dinner, so don't pull her over," I said and giggled.

"Okay, that's a wise thing to do," he said as he laughed. "See you soon. Be safe."

I hung up and smiled. "Be safe," I said out loud. I loved when he said that to me. *Another way of him taking care of me*, I thought.

As I stumbled through the dark apartment, I could see that Annie had gone out of her way, putting a few snacks in my empty candy bowls.

The girls were going to love her even more. I had to hurry. I ran a brush through my hair, applied the sensual lip gloss he loved, and thought about my outfit. I had to go with the little black dress. I smiled at myself in the mirror once I was ready. I had done all this in record time!

>─◆>─◦─<◆─◄

I drove like crazy, handed the keys to the valet, pulled my short dress down a little, and smiled at the look I got from the kid parking cars. He had probably seen more than he should have. I spotted Mike as soon as I entered the restaurant. As I headed toward him, I stumbled a bit in my new strappy high-heeled shoes.

"Your dinner is cold," Mike scolded as he stood to greet me.

"I hurried as fast as I could," I stammered, but I noticed there were no plates on the table. I smiled at him as he pulled out my chair. "Cute, babe. Cute!"

"I waited a few minutes to order. I knew you would take a little longer than twenty minutes." He smiled, returning to his chair.

"Not much," I said, grabbing his hand and noting the time on his watch.

"You look good. It was worth the wait."

"Thanks," I said, blushing. "How was your afternoon?"

"Hmm, so-so, I guess."

That was the extent of his response. What else had I expected?

A server arrived and set our salads in front of us. *Ugh!* I thought. *Now our nice romantic dinner has to be rushed.* As soon as I had that thought, it was replaced with the thought of how selfish I was being, knowing his mom was gravely ill, and he needed to get back to her.

"Are you looking forward to the girls getting here?" he said, breaking into my thoughts.

"Yes, I just wish you and I had more time. It seems we don't ever have the time we plan. Something always goes wrong on someone's end. I guess that's the life we live, right?" I questioned, wanting him to make it better.

"Yes, but at least you understand business. When things don't go exactly as planned, you don't get all bent out of shape. I do know that sometimes I need to make up for thoughtless behavior. I am a stupid guy, right?"

Oh, if he only knew what was going on in my head most times he was late or canceled, I thought.

Our dinner arrived on cue. I looked over at this man sitting across from me and realized once again that he was so much like me. He always thanked the server and never, ever complained about his food. Most men of his status would have found something to fuss about, but he was always grateful. I loved that about him!

Like most people, Mike ate faster than I did. I liked to savor every bite. So this evening's dinner, like most, he finished before me.

"You ready?" he asked when he was done.

"Huh? I guess I am!" I intentionally placed my knife and fork down, parallel to each other, to indicate that I had finished. I slowly picked up my napkin, patting my lips as he came around to get my chair. I stood up and casually placed the napkin on the table.

We walked out to the parking lot, and I noticed many eyes appeared to be on us. A few guys did double takes. "Hey, hey, Mike who's the blonde?" someone called out.

"Business, guys. Business. Besides, she's too young," he said with a smile.

"Okay, I guess I'll see you tomorrow," I said hesitantly as we neared my car.

"Hell no! C'mon, get into my car," he insisted. He had driven one of his toys—a '67 Corvette. He opened the passenger door and gestured for me to get in. "Let's go for a short drive, Ms. Malone."

"Of course, your wish is my command, sir." I slipped into the passenger seat. I loved sports cars. Something else we had in common—a love for fast cars with great-looking rear ends!

He turned on the car and blasted the stereo. *Oh, Mr. Boss, you know what I like*, I thought. The engine vibrated my whole seat, but I really couldn't hear it over the sound of the music. We took off into the night. His hand found its way off the shifter and onto my thigh. He turned down the music. "You okay?" he asked.

"Oh yes," I answered. "Definitely yes." I smiled, looking up at the quarter moon that was shining orange in the sky. "Babe, look at the moon. Do you see the moon?" I asked loudly.

"Yes, it is gorgeous." He sped around the corners and through the dips in the road. The car certainly handled like a dream, hugging the road the way Mr. Boss hugged my body when we were in the throes of passion.

"You sure you're okay?" he inquired again.

I just squeezed his hand.

He smiled and then gunned it. I loved the speed and being a little reckless. We pulled up to a familiar place, but I was out of sorts in the dark. He got out and came to open my door.

"Come on," he instructed.

"Wait, we are at your house?" I halfway asked as I saw the garage door open.

"Uh-huh," he said as he ducked under the door before it was fully up.

"Mike, wait. What about your daughter?"

"She is out of town for the next few days." He opened the door from the garage to the house, led me in, and closed it behind me.

I kicked off my heels and felt his hand behind my head and his breath on my face. He gently kissed my lips, the same gentle kiss I had felt on my lips all those months ago on that cold sidewalk outside the spa. Before I knew it, he had his arm under my legs and was picking me up.

"Babe, you can't ..." Too late. We were already headed to the bedroom.

He placed me down on the bed and kissed me deeply. "Sorry, but we have to make this quick," he said. "I have to meet my sister at the hospital to switch off. She needs to get home to her kids," he said, taking off his shirt and my breath away with it.

I quickly threw my dress to the side, and he kissed me deeper and longer than he ever had. I loved this more romantic side of things. His strong hands grabbed my breasts, and as his lips left mine, I knew exactly where they were going. I moaned. I wanted this to be anything but quick. But I would enjoy what I got.

"Babe, I miss you even when we are together. Does that sound silly?" I asked.

"Silly? Is there anything silly about us?"

I felt his tongue wander down my stomach and stop at my navel, where he nibbled some more. "I have been waiting to take you like this. Are you okay?" he asked.

"I'm okay," I managed to say.

We had talked about this on the phone, and I'd known this was going to happen, but was I ready? I didn't have time to wonder long. Oh my god, yes, that was the spot.

"Uhh," I uttered. "Oh, Mike, oh my god." I felt his tongue slowly caressing what we had nicknamed "Georgia" in our phone conversations.

I was moaning outside of myself again. I heard it, but it was like someone else was making the noise. I heard him moaning too, enjoying having me this way as much as I enjoyed taking him in my mouth.

I found myself so into the moment. I placed my hand on the hand he had inside of me, while my other hand fondled my breast. I was thrown into a climax, but he kept on Georgia until I thought I would explode, and then I did. I screamed out in pleasure. Then he slid up on top of me.

"How was that, baby?" he asked, grinning.

"Oh my god, incredible!" I guided him into me. From the first thrust, I was holding back a climax. Slowly, he slid in and out. I put my hands on his hips to stop him. I moved my hips in a curving downward motion so he was hitting every bit of me.

"Uh-uh-uh," he moaned.

"You like that, baby?" I whispered.

"Oh yeah, you?" he questioned.

"Oh yes, I'm about to go again," I moaned.

"Let me know, baby. I'll go with you," he groaned.

A couple more thrusts, and I felt the moistness of our lovemaking and our thighs sliding together.

"Now, baby, now!" I moaned.

"Keep it going, baby. Keep it going," he instructed.

I kept up the same movement, moving my hips in an up-and-down fashion, but more down and away from him, so he slipped way out. Then I gave a few circular motions when I heard him groan loudly.

"Holy fuck, baby, I'm gonna go." He climaxed but kept moving. He could tell I hadn't gone again.

"C'mon, baby, come on," he whispered. "Just love me now," he said as he looked into my eyes. Then with one final thrust he was deep into me. He looked at me with love, no desire and no lust. He then moved very slowly with short movements. "Whenever you're ready. I'm ready to go with you."

Oh my god, my feet were hot, my legs were tingling, and I climaxed. We were truly making love. It was Mike and me now—no Mr. Boss, no "business comes first," no daughters, no outside crap. Neither one of us was dominant. It was just us, and we were in love. I saw a vulnerable man in his eyes. All those emotions were all I could take, and tears fell from my eyes.

"I love you, baby. Shit, do I love you," he said loudly.

When our bodies stopped trembling, I held his face to mine. "I love you too, Mike. I love you too."

He wiped the tears from my face and smiled. "Sorry, sweetie. We have to get going."

And so it went with us.

>─!─◆>─○─<�◆─!─<

"Welcome to New York," I said with a smile as the two most beautiful girls came down the escalator at the Albany airport. It was late, and I was exhausted, but I was so glad to see my babies.

"Ah, what, wait, where are we?" said Sarah, acting as though she were sleepwalking.

Zoe just smiled and gave me a hug. "Where's my bed, Mom?"

"C'mon, let's get you two comfortable. Wait until you see our home away from home. It is great. We have a huge pool, a gym, a place that offers weekly yoga, and a huge big-screen TV for us to watch our Lifetime movies."

We piled into the car, and within thirty minutes, we arrived at the apartment complex. The girls were far too weary to make any comments. They stumbled in with their luggage and within minutes had found their beds and collapsed.

I kissed them each good night and told them how good it felt that they were with me. I reminded them that there was plenty of food if they woke up hungry.

"Good, Mom. I love you," Zoe said sleepily.

"What sort of food y …?" Sarah started to ask, but travel fatigue took over. "I love ya, Mom."

"Try to get some sleep, I'm going to bed also. It has been a long day. You'll find what you need in the kitchen, and tomorrow you will see your mom in action. I'm presenting to about one hundred people on how to be a spa owner."

I turned off their lights; they were already asleep. My babies were back with me, and that warmed my heart. My heart had worked over-time that day!

CHAPTER 16

Finding a Buyer

"Aloha. I hope you are all enjoying the light snacks, or as we say in the islands, *pupus*, that we have put out for you," I said, beginning my sales pitch.

"Most of you are here because you have an interest in ownership of a New Age day spa. State-of-the-art massage therapy relates not only to youth and health, but also to our mental well-being—the mind, body, and spirit. Some of you are here because you are regular clients of Herbal Essence Longevity Inc. You have shown interest in learning more about ownership in that regard, and yet others are just here for our Hawaiian delight, the *pupus*." I had tried to make a joke, but nobody laughed.

"Nonetheless, we are all here for an hour or so of boring—uh, I mean clever—salesmanship." My second joke failed too, so I instructed myself to tell no more. "How do we bring the aloha spirit to life in New York? Let's get started." Hawaiian music was gently playing in the background, and I spoke for the next forty-five minutes, using my graphs, photos, and product advertisements. I passed the products around for some to sample. Meanwhile, out of the corner of my eye, I saw my two beautiful children there to cheer on Mom. I felt lucky.

I had often wondered whether my children would take an interest in business. If it was the construction business or other businesses I had a part in, that would be nice. I even saw them in different careers within the business. Zoe would be great at management, and Sarah would excel at accounting. I smiled and continued my presentation.

"We can clearly see the need for lifestyle improvements that warrant these services, which of course will increase our revenue. This is not a million-dollar overnight business. This is a business. I want someone who knows what it takes to run a business and not be afraid of the downs—a person who will work through them, because that's what it will take to grow." The audience applauded. "Even as I say these words, I see the scared looks on a few faces, and even those who don't show it feel it, I'm sure. I know there are many who are thinking what I thought—this is a great opportunity! You must have fear. That's normal as long as you don't let it paralyze you.

"I once had a professor who said to me, 'Miss Malone, are you going to sink or swim?' Well, of course, I answered, 'Swim.' 'Wrong,' he retorted. 'You will always sink a little at first, and maybe a lot; then you will swim! But only if you are well prepared and willing to take the good with the bad. Take criticism from all and mostly learn, learn, learn, then apply.'"

I pointed to a woman in the back row who had been showing great interest. "Are you going to sink or swim?" I asked her, loudly enough to get the attention of the gentleman in the back who had eaten one too many *pupus* and was thinking it was nap time. *Not on my time, it's not*, I thought.

"If you're up to holding your breath with me for a little while, until we can swim and find our yacht together"—I looked around and smiled—"then my e-mail address is up on this last slide. Or you can stop by the spa. I will be here all week. Let's visit about this awesome opportunity."

Applause rang out in the room, and the buzz of excited chatter was overwhelming. I looked over at Annie, who had a big smile of approval on her face. I could she was now ready to move in like a shark with her info packets to follow up.

The girls quickly approached me. "That was great, Mom. You are awesome," Zoe said. She had become my biggest fan. Sarah was a close second; I knew young men were starting to get in her way.

"Does this mean no more visits to New York for us?" whined Sarah.

"We'll see. You never know what the future holds, baby, that's for sure," I told her. No truer words had I ever spoken. "How about we get some takeout and watch one of those Lifetime movies I have been bragging about recording for us?"

"Sounds good, Mom!" Sarah said enthusiastically.

"Yeah, I'm so jet-lagged," Zoe chimed in.

"How lame are we?" I said with a laugh.

"But we are cute," Sarah giggled.

"Aha, that we are. That we are."

My buzzing phone took our attention. Sarah and I looked down simultaneously to see Mike's name on the screen.

"Who's that, Mom?" Zoe asked

"Mike!" Sarah responded.

"I have to take this. Mike probably wants to know how the meeting went. Why don't you guys call and order whatever you want from our favorite place? I'll take this call, and then we'll go pick it up." I stepped outside to answer my phone. "Hey, you."

"Hey, you yourself. How are the girls?"

"So tired, but they'll be fine in a few days."

"How was the meeting?"

"It was good. I think we may have a few good prospects. I'll know more next week. Annie is in there encouraging who she can," I reassured him.

"Yeah, well, I'll keep my fingers crossed. Meanwhile, I have a gal wanting to meet with you next week. Her husband owns a lumberyard down south, so they definitely have the money."

"That's great, Mike."

"She was a business major with a little background over the years, but I think they are serious. They have two kids, and she is busy with them. Wednesday was her only day. I said that would be good. I hope that's okay," Mike said.

"That's great. I have the state board walking through Wednesday, though. Maybe I can meet her at your construction office first and then take her to the spa once they are gone?"

"Uh, yeah, that's fine. Here, let me give you her number. Her name is Taylor, and you can set it all up. I told her you had other prospects, so hopefully that lights a fire."

"Yeah, well, we'll see."

"What are you doing now? Can I see you?" he asked hopefully.

"Ah, I'm going to get takeout with the girls and watch a movie," I said, not wanting to sound disappointed because I had missed my girls. "What are you doing?" I wanted him to say "longing for you."

"I'm headed to see my mom."

"How is she?" I asked.

"As well as can be expected, I guess." He seemed emotionless.

"I'm sorry, babe," I stuttered as I saw Sarah approaching. "Hey, Sarah, did you get dinner ordered?" I asked loudly to let Mike know she was there and could hear us talking.

"Oh, the girls are there? Okay, I'll let you go. Try to call me later, please," he said in his polite voice.

"Yes, okay, Mike. I will definitely call Taylor and set up the meeting," I said in my business voice so that the girls wouldn't catch on.

"What are we picking up for dinner?" I asked, putting my phone away.

It was so good to have the evening with the girls. It seemed like I hadn't seen them in forever. We watched our movie and made fun of the bad acting while talking about boys, next year's class schedules, and jobs.

"Oh, Sarah, put down your phone for two minutes!" Zoe screamed.

"Zoe, someday you will be there, so don't be so critical," I said.

She shot me a "no way" look.

"Guaranteed, Zoe," I said.

"Oh, Mom," she said, "anyway, why does she even like him? He doesn't even play sports." At that time Zoe and Sarah were very much into hockey and other sports. So Zoe got perturbed when her sister dated someone who didn't have the same likes.

I could see Sarah growing up before my eyes, and I knew Zoe was right behind her. They were going to grow up, have their own lives, and make Mom proud, of course. Then I was forced to think about what I would be doing. I realized I needed to start making decisions for my life.

"That was one of the dumbest movies yet," Sarah laughed.

"Yes, Sarah, we are already over it," Zoe said.

"But we do agree?" I said, trying to ease the tension. I tackled them on the couch, and we all start giggling and wrestling around.

"Hey, wait a minute," I called out. "We have to go see the fireflies. I am so excited to show you the fireflies."

"What on earth is a firefly, Mom?" Sarah asked.

"They are the greatest, and you just have to see for yourself."

"Well, whatever it is that has you willing to leave a mess behind, I have to see for myself," Zoe said.

"I don't know how long the fireflies are out, but I think Sarah said that she would clean up when we got home," I teased.

"Wait, what? No, I didn't!" exclaimed Sarah.

"I'm in then," quipped Zoe.

"I can't wait for you to see them. I researched on the Internet, but I couldn't find solid info on why their butts light up," I said, smiling mysteriously.

"What? Their butts light up?" Zoe said, laughing. "I gotta see this."

I took them to a place Clare had told me about. We waited patiently, and in a few moments we began seeing little flashes in the dark. We sat in the cool night air in awe of our new little friends, until the mosquitoes realized there was fresh meat available.

"Thanks, Mom," Sarah cooed as we pulled away. "That was really great."

"Yeah," Zoe agreed.

I just smiled as we pulled back into traffic.

"Ha-ha! Sarah has to clean up when we get home," Zoe sang.

"Why, you little brat ..."

They both began to giggle.

>─┤◆>─◯─◇┤─<

Wednesday rolled around, and business was booming at the spa. Annie was in charge and doing a fine job as always. So I headed off to Mike's construction office to meet my new prospect.

"Hey, Tia."

"Hi, Clare. I have a meeting with a gal named Taylor today. I guess she is married to a lumber guy or something?" I said.

"Oh yes, she is ... they are very well off. Not sure if she could run the spa. She seems a little spoiled if you ask me."

I didn't ask you, I thought, but I smiled. I guessed I was tired of everybody's two cents when I was doing all the work.

A petite, well-dressed brunette walked in. She definitely looked like she visited a health and beauty spa regularly; her skin was flawless.

"Hello," she said cheerily. "I'm supposed to meet with Tia Malone."

"Yes, hello. I am Tia," I said, holding out my hand. I was hoping for a nice firm handshake, but even when I gripped a little harder, she didn't comply.

She was pleasant enough, but as the conversation led into revenue, it seemed to me she was seeking something a little more lucrative. I offered to take her on a tour of the spa, but she declined. She left on a good note and told me she would call the next day.

Taylor never called back, as I had expected. By the end of the week, I was feeling discouraged enough to cry. Every meeting went the same way—everyone wanted either a promissory earnings statement or a buyback clause.

Monday morning, I had a most encouraging meeting. The gentleman was well versed in business, he checked out financially, and he was ready to go immediately. We had a few more legal items to go over regarding the takeover, and he agreed to meet again the end of the week.

Before he left, I suggested that we go into the spa and meet Annie. We had already discussed the business help package that included Annie staying on board. I made the introductions, and he started asking her questions. It seemed they didn't need me any longer, so I excused myself, letting him know I would contact the landlord regarding the lease and set up a time for them to meet. I was relieved.

I called Mike to tell him the good news and schedule the necessary meeting.

"Certainly, no problem. Just say the day and time, and I'll have you both come to my office."

"Thanks, Mike. I feel pretty positive about this one if he checks out completely. He is with Annie as we speak, and they seem to get along very well. I am going to meet with him to finalize the sale next week after the girls leave. He wants me here for one week of training, and then he's good with Annie. I promised I'd check in with him weekly over the telephone. It's all working out perfectly!"

"That's great. I'm proud of you, Tia." I sensed his insecurity over knowing the end was near. "Can we try to grab an hour together tonight at my place? After you are done with the girls, of course? I'm really needing you by my side." He sounded sad.

"Yes, of course. As a matter of fact, the girls are going to a concert tonight. I have to drop them off and pick them up afterward."

"Great, Tia. Come over after you leave them. That will be around eight, right? God, I can't wait to hold you."

"Me too, babe. I miss you always."

>─┼◀▸─○─◂▸┼─◀

Back in the spa, Richard Moore and Annie had been going over more than I had expected, and he was most happy. I thought I felt a little something else between them too. I walked Richard out, and we planned on meeting in two days.

Back at the apartment, the girls could instantly see how good I felt.

"You sold the spa, didn't you?" Sarah called out from the couch, where she was watching television.

"As a matter of fact, it looks like it is in the bag, not 100 percent, but almost!"

"Great work, Mom," Zoe said, but I could tell she was more interested in the show they were watching.

"I'm going to freshen up a little before I drop you off at the concert," I told them. "It's been a long day, and I still have to meet with Mike regarding the lease. I have a meeting with him scheduled while you are at the concert. I'll pick you up as planned around 10:00 p.m."

>─┼◀▸─○─◂▸┼─◀

We stopped to grab a quick bite to eat on the way to the concert, and as we were sitting in the restaurant, Sarah suddenly asked, "Where did you say you were going tonight?"

"I have to take care of the new buyer and his lease, so I'm meeting with Mike," I said casually.

"Looking like that?" Zoe said.

"What do you mean?" I said defensively. "I'm not dressed any different than when I go to my office," I retorted nervously.

"No, it's not that. You are dressed casual, but kind of sexy, and boy, you smell good. You sure you are not falling for this guy?" Zoe giggled.

"Oh, Zoe, why would you think that?"

"Probably because of the look on your face. You are blushing, Mom," Sarah added.

"Mom, I agree with her, and he is kind of cute for an older guy," Zoe said, getting bashful.

"Well, you don't have to worry. It is strictly business. Come on now. Finish up and let me drop you at the concert."

>─┼◄▸•─O─•◄▸┼─◄

That had been close, and I knew I was blushing. I had indeed picked out something sexy, and yes, I had put a little extra perfume on in all the right places. I smiled and then even laughed a little, knowing that I couldn't put much over my girls.

I arrived at Mr. Boss's house and rang the doorbell. He opened the door immediately, grabbed me, pulled me in, and steered me into the bedroom. He started by kissing my neck and telling me how hot I'd made him when he saw me in his office.

The sound of his voice, the smell of his cologne, and the way his hot breath felt on my neck took me to a place of pure pleasure even before the kissing began. He had a way of activating all my senses simultaneously.

He undressed me slowly and kissed every inch of my upper body, and then without reservation he pushed me down on the bed. I looked up into his brown eyes, and we held our gaze much longer than usual. I grabbed his hands, pulled him down on me, and then motioned for him to roll over onto his back. I took the back of his head into my hand and grabbed his hair, pulling enough to pull his head back. His mouth dropped open, and I took his lips into my mouth. I bit down softly yet firmly enough that he knew who was in control. I continued biting at his neck.

"I think about you all day every day," I whispered. "I can't wait to have your hardness inside my warm body, but before that can happen, you must pay for a few things you've done wrong, baby," I teased.

"Oh yeah, what have I done wrong?" he asked innocently.

"Well, you know the punch list on the job site?"

"Yes, I do."

"It's kind of like that. Pretty long, lots of little things, but none no less important than another, and they all need to be dealt with. So we are just going to deal with them now and call it even. Is that good with you?"

"I'm okay with that, babe." He sounded a bit confused, not knowing what he was in for.

"You just relax, baby." I laid my body completely on his, stretching my arms to meet his hands. I took his mouth hard against mine and plunged my tongue deep into his mouth. I felt him gasp, but I didn't let up. I grabbed his head so he couldn't move away from me. I bit his lower lip, but not causing any pain, just pleasure. I took his tongue into my mouth, imitating the way I sucked him. I felt his body tense beneath mine.

I moved my mouth to his ear and whispered how much I needed him to give it to me, but only when I said and when I was ready. I told him if he was bad, he would only be teased like this. I asked him firmly if he understood.

"Ah yeah, baby," he whispered. I could tell he would explode the minute I let him enter me.

"Turn over," I commanded. He did as I instructed. I kissed his muscular back all the way down to his well-rounded behind. I bit down hard enough to hear him whimper a few times.

I was so turned on that I thought I would climax before he entered me. My body was moving all over his as my lips caressed his butt all the way down to his manhood. I continued loving every part of his body. He reached back and tried to touch me again, but I shoved his hand away.

"No, not yet! I will let you know when it is okay to pleasure your lady."

I couldn't control myself, so I began to touch myself. I was so wet and warm—*yes, a woman wanting her man*, I thought.

"God, baby, I have to have you. Please?" he begged.

I moved so he could flip over into a position from which he could take me. He moved on top of me, and I heard him groan. Just before he entered me, I slipped out from underneath him.

"What the fuck?" he said.

I turned toward the foot of the bed, and my mouth surrounded him. I parted my legs to allow him to take me into his mouth. He didn't.

"Can I take you, please?" he said.

I didn't answer; I just moved closer to his mouth. Our bodies moved in nature's dance. We made love until we couldn't exert any more energy.

Lying still beside him, I knew I had to get going. "Shower?" I asked.

"Shower," he answered, smiling. "How are we doing for time?" he asked.

"Perfect! We timed that perfectly." *The girls will never know,* I thought, *or will they?* Surely I would appear different after having had my body ravished.

I gathered my clothes and practically ran through the shower. I checked myself in the mirror quickly to make certain everything was back in place. "Ready," I said as I headed out the bathroom and toward the front door.

"Will I see you again?" he joked.

"Well, I don't know if my father would approve," I giggled.

"Come here, you little brat," he said, grabbing me. "I love you."

"I love you too, but now I have to go."

We kissed good-bye, and I quickly left to pick up the girls.

When I picked them up, they reported that the concert was even better than they'd thought it would be. We drove home while they told me about the entire concert.

Time had certainly flown by. The next few days, I spent entirely with the girls before they left. I planned to stay a little longer to tie up loose ends.

"I feel sad, Mom. We leave tomorrow," Zoe said, almost in tears.

"I know, Zoe, but I am going to be home twelve days behind you. Then you know what happens, right?"

"What? Oh yeah, a new semester of school starts ..." She scowled.

"No. Clothes shopping," I said, poking at her.

She smiled. "Oh yeah, awesome!"

"Oh yes, and I want to get a new swimsuit," Sarah said.

Clothes shopping for every semester of school was another of our mother-daughter traditions. We would buy an entire wardrobe on a two-day trip to Oahu (there were not many options for shopping on Maui). Of course, I took them separately, so my school shopping stretched out into two weekends. I never complained, though. I loved getting to know them on our school shopping trips. They would talk about friends, classes, teachers, and the everyday life of a teenager.

"I have so much to do. I have to change a few classes and fix up my room to accommodate my new schedule," Zoe stated, a little more excited.

"Oh, Zoe, you kill me," I said, smiling. "Are you two just about packed?"

"Of course, Zoe is, so can she help me," Sarah said.

We all laughed.

⊱┈✦┈◯┈✦┈⊰

"Good morning, Annie," I said, rushing in.

"Good morning, Tia. Running a little late this morning? Today is the big day with Mr. Moore," she said with a smile, and I noticed that she looked particularly pretty that day.

"Yes, I had to drop the girls off, and the plane was a little late leaving, and so it goes. Any messages?"

"No, nothing this morning."

"Can you please make sure all the paperwork is in order for my meeting? All the legal paperwork should be on my desk already."

"Yes, the legal paperwork is on your desk. I didn't open it. All the other documents, I was waiting on to print. I wanted to make certain all the name spellings were correct. I can take that off the legal work if you'd like. Then it will all be ready when he gets here."

"Yes, Annie, that would be great." I smiled, feeling gratitude and relief. I had ten minutes until the scheduled meeting time.

Ten minutes later, he had not arrived. *On time is late, and he is late,* I thought. Another ten minutes passed. *Ten minutes late is shamefully late! He is shamefully late!*

I peeked around the corner and saw Annie sitting at her desk.

"Any calls?" I questioned.

"No," she said, frowning. "He's probably just running late." She was trying to reassure me, but I heard the disappointment in her voice.

An hour later, there was still no Mr. Moore.

"Annie, can you give him a call and see what is keeping him? Please tell him I have a schedule to keep."

"Yes, right away." A few minutes later, I heard her voice on the intercom. "There is no answer, Tia. Sorry."

He hadn't called, and he hadn't shown up; I was left feeling a little sick to my stomach.

"I am so sorry, Tia," Annie said, trying to console me, as I exited my office.

"I'm sorry for you as well. I think you two clicked."

"Yes, I thought so too. Always hoping," she said with a smile. "One must not give up on anything."

I just smiled and headed out the door to my lonely apartment. I hated the thought of walking in there without the girls.

After three more days of meeting prospective buyers and finding no real interest, I still hadn't heard from Mr. Moore. I searched for him, of course, but it was almost like he had been in my imagination.

By day six, I realized Mr. Moore had taken advantage of the situation to retrieve proprietary information. Annie and I had given it all away too, not even thinking twice. He was smooth, that Mr. Moore! I felt used, not to mention stupid. There I was with no buyer and no prospects, and I was leaving in a few days. Maybe the worst part about it was I had to tell Mike. I had to tell him I was leaving with no plans of returning, and the spa was closing. I cried myself to sleep again that night.

Don't be dismayed by good-byes. A farewell is necessary before you can meet again. And meeting again, after moments or lifetimes, is certain for those who are friends.

—Richard Bach

CHAPTER 17

Parting Is Such Sweet Sorrow

looked down at my phone. Mike was calling. I couldn't take his call just yet. I needed to finish burning off the bad energy of the last few days in this intense workout I was in the middle of. It was almost painful to hit the ignore button on him. But I was hoping this workout would get my serotonin flowing again.

I finished my workout feeling completely drained and headed home to shower. I called Mike on the way.

"Hey, babe, I was just about to call you," he said.

"Well, great minds think alike," I said, managing my first smile of the day.

"Yes, they do." I could envision his smile as I heard his comeback.

Sometimes I couldn't believe how alike we were. We were perfect for each other. Where our personalities differed, they actually complemented each other. I loved and missed the long talks we had about life in general when I was six thousand miles away. When I was there, we tried to shove all we could get into that limited time. I thought we had become closer because of the distance.

"Two peas in a pod, we are, sweetie," he told me affectionately.

"What are you doing, babe?"

"Just headed out to look at potential development. Want to ride along?" he suggested.

"A construction site?" I perked up. I loved being out on construction sites. I loved the smells, the sounds, the changing earth. "I have to shower. I'm just leaving the gym. Pick me up at the apartment in a half hour?" I asked.

"See you then."

Crud, I thought, *I hope I packed work jeans. Can't ruin a Calvin Klein suit on a job site. I wasn't expecting to be in the dirt this trip. I'll make something work, though.*

In no time I was ready to roll. I heard his truck pull up, and I bounded out the door.

He smiled.

"What?" I asked as I opened the door.

"Well, just wondering why you're so happy. It's not like I brought you candy and flowers. We are just going to look at a job."

"You should know by now this is more exciting for me than a romantic meal out—well, most days. Where are we going?" I asked like a little kid.

He laughed. "There's that silly side of you! Haven't seen it in a while ... been kind of stressful, huh? We are headed out to the prairie off Route 9. There's an old golf course I am thinking of buying and bringing back to its glory, if I can get the acreage around it permitted for housing."

"Hmm, you amaze and inspire, Mr. Mike."

As we rode, we talked about the girls and about his daughter. We talked about his mom and even our relationships with our parents. I smiled. I just knew this was the man for me. It was a long, hot afternoon, and I enjoyed every minute. My two favorite things to talk about were construction and Mr. Boss!

We drove through a few of his other projects on the way back into town and got some pretty funny looks from his job site managers. He stopped and spoke to a few employees. I loved his no-nonsense, get-it-done type of talk when it came to his employees and his subcontractors. They knew if they didn't get it right, there was someone else waiting to do the work for this man. So when he called, they answered. He showed his gratitude by working the best men as much as he could.

"Who's this, your latest?" one man joked.

"Uh, no, this is my state inspector," he stated.

"Yeah right, Mike. You get all the women; you should leave some for the rest of us," he teased.

We drove away, and I thought about saying something. But what? I knew how job-site talk went. I thought about all the crazy things probably said about me by my employees. I told myself to stop being insecure.

"Are you hungry? Want to do dinner?" he asked.

"Yes. I could eat a little something, although I should probably be starving myself."

He just smiled, and I could tell he was thinking about something. I reached for his hand and squeezed it.

"What are you thinking about?" I asked.

"What if you and I were to do a job together?" he said, glancing at me.

"Well," I said, thinking quickly, "I think we could do great things together. I mean, we do think alike. We would definitely know what the other was thinking and doing most of the time." *That was a stupid answer*, I thought.

At the restaurant, we were shown to a booth, and I slid in. Mike grimaced as he sat down across from me.

"You okay, babe?"

"Yeah, just my back acting up again. Nothing a little back rub couldn't help," he said, grinning.

This gave me an opportunity to bring up the spa situation. "I have some grim news regarding that buyer I was so excited about," I blurted out quickly.

He looked less than thrilled. I took a deep breath and tried to get a handle on my own disappointment.

A singsong voice broke in. "What's for lunch?" the server asked.

"I'll have the special," Mike answered.

"I'll have the same," I said as I handed her my menu. "So anyway," I continued, "he is missing in action. I have done a lot of checking, and it seems as though Mr. Moore was just getting information for his own business. I should have spotted this, but all my initial checking on him came out positive. I'm not quite sure where I went wrong. Maybe it was my desperation to sell the business and not close it down. Nonetheless,

I have no buyers." I looked down at my water glass in defeat and waited for his reaction.

I felt his hand on mine. "Hon, don't be so hard on yourself. You did all your checks, right?"

I nodded my head.

"Then you did nothing wrong. Sometimes things don't work out. Sometimes no matter how good we are at sealing every little crack, a little sludge slips in," Mike said, trying to comfort me.

"Mike, the truth is that I am more disappointed because of us. What will happen to us?"

"It's okay, Tia. It is what it is! Some things are sent to test us. The spa will be closed down, and I will find another tenant." He smiled awkwardly. He knew that was the least of my concerns. "But sweetie, what I won't find is another you, someone I have grown to love and was certain of seeing every few weeks or months." He looked to me for an answer.

We sat in silence for what seemed like forever.

"You are a good man, Mike. I don't want to lose you. But six thousand miles is a long way to maintain a relationship," I said with a defeated attitude.

"Especially with all the responsibilities we both have tearing us apart." He sighed and let go of my hand to make room for the food that was arriving.

"Thanks," we both said in unison as the server put our plates in front of us.

We both sat in silence, staring at our food, looking for answers. We had to talk about this. I had lost my appetite, and it looked like the man sitting across from me had lost his as well.

"What are our options?" Mike asked, shoving his plate away from him. "You come here, or I go there. Neither of us can do that. Do we put our relationship on hold?"

"How the heck do we do that, Mike? How do we just resume our lives like we haven't happened? I don't want a relationship over the telephone, and I'm sure you don't either. How do I not feel you, smell you, and taste you?"

Mike raised his hand for me to stop. "I feel the same way, babe. It pisses me off that we have no freedom to be with each other. I truly love you."

"But not enough for you to uproot yourself and live in Hawaii?"

"Tia, how could I? That is not fair. My business, my mom, my daughter?"

"Stop! I know. Mike, please don't remind me. Life is not fair!" I said, frustrated. My eyes were welling up with tears.

"Well, do you love me enough to uproot yourself and come live in New York?" he countered.

"Mike, you know I can't—my girls, my business." I looked away as the tears began to spill onto my cheeks. I felt Mike's hand lift mine to his lips.

"It is not whether we love each other enough that decides what we do," he said gently. "We both know what we have and will always have. There is no time limit on this."

"I know, Mike. I know."

"There is no answer. Sometimes, Tia, we are sent obstacles that seem daunting. We have to remember that we are never sent anything too big for us to handle."

"You are right. Thank you, sweetie." I smiled and picked up my napkin to wipe away my defeatist tears. Suddenly I was feeling much better. Nervously, I asked, "Babe, remember that little saying: If you love something, set it free. If it comes back, it's yours; if not, it was never meant to be?"

"Tia, all we can do is know that we love each other and want to be together. Today if that isn't possible, it's because other people need us. It's not letting go," he said, looking so deeply into my eyes that I felt he could see my soul. "We'll both be okay."

I knew why he had been put in my life. He had awakened my body and spirit; he had allowed me to overcome my fears. He'd taught me to give my mind and body totally, to learn and know that the love and intimacy shared between a man and a woman was beautiful. If I had not met Mr. Boss, I never would have known that.

I gave a big sigh of relief.

"Clare and I plan on hitting the city one last time before I leave tomorrow," I said right out of the blue.

He smiled at me as if to say, *You are such a girl, but I love you anyway.* "Are you going for the day or overnight?"

"Just the day," I responded, smiling.

"Oh, that's good. I want to have you every night before you leave."

"I know. Me too. How's your food?"

"I'm done. It looked great, but my appetite was fulfilled in another way. What about yours?" he asked as he motioned to my plate with his fork.

"Great, but the company became my meal, and it was better than great." I smiled and put my leg over his.

He smiled back. God, that smile and those eyes.

Why had I ever told Clare I would go shopping for the entire day tomorrow? I wished I could take it back. But I had promised the girls a few things from the city that we couldn't get at home, so I couldn't take it back.

"You okay?" he said, interrupting my thoughts.

"Uh, yeah, just rethinking my shopping trip with Clare."

"Why would you not want to go?" He grinned knowingly.

"Um, I don't know ... maybe a little thing named Mike."

"What are you shopping for anyway?"

"The girls saw a few things last time they were in the city at a little shop that they just can't live without—you know, things we can't get on Maui. I promised I would stop in the city before I got back."

"Well then, you have to go. I would never want you to exchange time with me for something you promised your girls. That would be selfish of me, and also I have become very fond of those two girls."

Sometimes I couldn't believe I was so lucky to be involved with this man. He was so kind, generous, and caring, once you got past the initial rough and tough exterior. There were times I wished the world could see this side of him, but I understood the need for the rough and tough act. I understood the need for the walls.

"You are so sweet," I said, smiling.

"Yeah, how sweet? Can I have a little extra tonight for being so sweet?"

Things were back on track, as they should've been, for our last few days before I left. I shook my head and knew that my face was already turning red.

"You are so cute, my little Miss Red Face," he said, laughing.

God, that laugh! I thought.

"Let's get out of here!" Mike said, signaling for the check.

⊱┈◈┈○┈◈┈⊰

Just as I crossed the threshold, his lips found mine.

"You were beautiful tonight, our talk, our honesty, the understanding and acceptance, but then you already know that, don't you?" he whispered as he held my head back slightly by my hair.

"Thank you" was all I could think to say. What I wanted to say was *Thank you for making me feel beautiful. Thank you for helping me become this woman who is completely whole. Thank you for making my knight in shining armor come to life and for teaching me how to rescue myself, all the while making me feel needed and necessary. Thank you for teaching me how to be calm, cool, and collected.* I smiled to myself. I was beautiful, and I was complete; I felt it inside and out. *Thank you, Mr. Boss. Thank you.*

I didn't even turn the lights out as he began undressing me. "You are way too good at that," I said teasingly.

"What?"

"Unhooking my bra."

"It's like riding a bike; you never forget."

I just smiled to myself and moaned a bit as he laid me down on the bed. I rolled on top of him and began kissing him. Gently, I ran my tongue down his chest, lingering to nibble in a few of my favorite places. I felt the desire pulsating through my body, yet my mind wouldn't stop asking, what if this was the last time we made love?

"Tonight, Mike, I want to make love. I want it to be slow and tender." I laid my head on my pillow.

He said nothing. He began kissing my mouth and then slowly ran his lips down my body, stopping as I had done in his favorite places. I tried touching him.

"Lay still," he said, before he buried his tongue in me. "You taste wonderful," he said and then went back to exploring me with his tongue. He purposely stayed away from Georgia, which drove me crazy. He knew it by my moans and continued to tease me.

"No more, no more. Take me, babe. Take me," I pleaded. He gently took Georgia with his mouth. I exploded almost instantly. He kept up his loving until I couldn't stand it any longer. I took hold of his head in both hands and pulled his willing body on top of mine.

"I love you, Tia. I love you. You are beautiful, and you are mine." He entered me slowly, almost as if he was teasing me.

"Oh god," I said, shivering. "I am about to go again."

"Go ahead, baby. I have you," he said in that deep sexy voice, as he lifted himself up so that he could watch the pleasure wash over me.

I grabbed his firm round butt and pulled him into me at the rhythm I needed.

"Let it go, babe," he whispered, looking into my eyes. "*I am* here. I've got you. Go again for me."

I succumbed to the pleasure and heard him say, "That's my girl. There you go. I got you."

I held him tight for a few seconds until I had stopped trembling. He could tell when I was ready to start again.

I began to move with him, faster and faster. I pulled his head up to see his face as he climaxed. I looked into his eyes. I moved my hands down his arms and then tightened my fingers around his hard biceps and held on. I felt his entire body tense up. I saw the muscles in his neck tighten and felt his biceps get even firmer. I felt him throbbing inside of me as he started moaning with pleasure. Then he collapsed onto me, and all I felt then was our hearts beating loudly together as his body gave off the occasional tremor.

"You are amazing. I will never forget this moment." Those were the only words I could get out.

"I will never forget you, Tia."

>·+·⟨›·◦·⟨›·+·⟨

"Hi, Clare," I sang out, entering the office. "Oh, hello, Mike. I didn't' see you sitting there."

"Well, I sure don't get the greeting Clare does." He sounded a little jealous.

Clare just laughed. "I'm all ready to go."

"Where are you two going?" Mike asked, trying to cover up for the fact that he already knew.

"Shopping, shopping!" said Clare. "Want us to bring you back anything?"

"No, I think I'm good. Be safe on the drive," he said in his bossy voice.

"Yes, Mike, we will," Clare said, rolling her eyes. She turned to me. "Let's take my car. I know the road better, and you get charged for extra mileage on your rental car."

"Sounds good," I said, looking over at Mike as we headed out the door. He winked and smiled.

Our trip into the city was filled with talk about our kids and life in general, including her marital issues. I had no advice to give her in that area. Lord knew my marriage had been very rocky during its last few years. I had learned to cut myself some slack over that. Mike had helped me with that. Heck, Mike had helped with things he didn't even know about!

"I thought we would park in the city somewhere and just utilize city transportation. Sound good?"

"Of course, you are the driver," I said, smiling at Clare.

>─┤◆>─O─<◆┤─<

After shopping for three hours, Clare finally gave in. "Oh my god, my feet are killing me."

"Maybe walking fifteen blocks wasn't a good call," I confessed. "It didn't sound that far. Anyway, sorry," I said and pulled out a chair for our bags.

"Can I get you ladies something to drink?" our server asked.

"Um, nothing for me yet," I said, picking up the menu to search for something refreshing.

"I'll have the raspberry ice tea," said Clare.

"Hmm, that sounds good. I'll have one too."

Clare stood up again. "Tia, I have to use the ladies' room."

I smiled at her and then grabbed my cell phone to call Mike once she had walked away.

"Hey, you," he said.

"Hey, you yourself," I said, situating my body so that I could see when Clare returned from the restroom. "I just wanted to let you know that we are safe in the city and have stopped for lunch."

"Where's Clare?"

"She just went to the restroom, so I've got to make this quick."

"Are you being productive?"

"Yes, sir! I got the girls all the things they wanted. I even picked up a few things I know they had been eyeing."

"That's good. Call me when you get back."

"Yes, Mr. Boss ... uh, got to go. Here comes Clare."

"Okay, love you."

"I love you," I managed to say before hanging up.

Our tea was delivered right as Clare was sitting down, which I hoped would pull her attention away from me putting my phone away.

"Who was that?" Clare questioned.

"Oh, just the girls," I lied. "This raspberry tea is really good and quite refreshing," I said, changing the subject.

Our conversation turned to Mike. Somehow with Clare it always did. I thought once again that she might suspect what was going on between Mike and me.

"Before Mike asked his ex-wife to marry him," she said, "he was dating six other women, and none of them had a clue." She sounded almost exited to know this information. "Matter of fact, she found out and left him for about two months before she agreed to come back and marry him."

"Why are you telling me this?" I asked, trying not to look uncomfortable.

"Just thought you should know."

"Why would I care?"

She didn't answer me and continued rambling on. "There were many times he was running around with other women, borrowing employees' cars so he wouldn't get caught with them. One of the complex managers tells stories of him calling up to see what apartments were empty, and they knew what he was doing. Mike is a real ladies' man."

"So I should know that why?" I asked.

"Just want to protect your feelings, that's all."

"My feelings?" I questioned. I felt numb and decided not to say anymore. I thought about how two-faced she was being. I felt like pulling her gossiping tongue right out of her head.

My head felt dizzy, and I wanted to cry. All of what she was telling me sounded so believable. Then I reminded myself how employees liked to gossip about the boss.

The drive back seemed twice as long as the ride into the city. Clare kept my mind off everything she had told me about Mike with her endless chatter. That was good because otherwise I might have just slumped down in the seat and wept. Finally, we arrived back at my car. "I had a great time, Clare," I said as I pulled my bags from her car and loaded them into mine.

"Anytime, Tia. If I don't see you again, take care of yourself and those girls." As she drove away, she put her head out the window and said, "Sorry about the closing of the spa. It was fun while it lasted, huh?"

Another crushing blow for the day, I thought as I slipped onto the cold leather seat of my rental car. I hurried back to the apartment, promising myself I wouldn't call Mike until I'd had time to sort out all the information that had been thrown at me that day.

When I answered my ringing phone back at my apartment, I tried not to sound like I was upset.

"Are you okay? You didn't call, and I was getting worried."

"Oh yes, sorry. I just have a lot on my mind."

"Like what?"

"Oh, nothing really. Clare told me all about you and your women today."

"Oh yeah, like what?" he said.

"Nothing really important. Can this wait until tomorrow? I'm really tired."

"No, I'm sorry. It can't. I will be right over. You sound upset."

He hung up before I could resist his coming over.

I saw his truck lights and opened the door for him.

He swept me into his arms, asking if I was okay.

"Yes, I told you I was fine. Just tired," I halfway snapped at him.

"Well, I'm here. Tell me what Clare had to say," he insisted.

I told him the horrible things that she'd said about him, his character, and his behavior. When I was finished, he just smiled.

"Why are you smiling?"

"Well, it is kind of flattering that people don't have anything better to do than make up stories about me."

"So it's all lies?"

"Well, I have to tell you. I did once have a little bit of a wild side with the ladies. I was young and free. But anything that happened was before I was married," he assured me.

"What about the women you had in the empty apartments and all of that?"

"I didn't have near as much fun as Clare thinks I did. I was totally faithful to my wife. I don't know what else to say."

"Nothing, I guess. I am just trying to take this all in."

"Look, everybody has a past. And frankly, everyone wasn't as good as you." He smiled.

"How dare you say that to me? That was hurtful, Mike."

"Sorry, but it's true, sweetie."

"I think she really suspects us. I feel like an idiot. You have always been a nonstop topic with her. Either she loves to gossip, or she is secretly in love with you."

"No, I just think she has nothing better to talk about, and gossip is good for the soul," he said, winking at me.

I looked into his eyes, and he held my gaze. "Okay," I said. "Mike, I don't care about your past personal life and any mistakes you may or may not have made. That was before me. I know that we don't know what lies ahead for us, and we cannot plan, predict, or ask anything of each other. I panicked hearing what she said, and I felt insecure."

"Oh, babe, remember that I love you." He took my hand.

"I am exhausted. Are you going to stay awhile?" I asked.

"No, I have to get home. My daughter has some friends over. I really should be there."

I walked him to the door without letting go of his hand.

"I can't believe I am leaving without having you," he said.

"Well, you can have me all day tomorrow if you want," I said with a smile.

"I love you." He squeezed my hand.

"I love you too."

⋊•⊱•◦•⊰•⋉

The next few days flew by, and soon it was time for me to pack up.

I had already packed up the boxes from the apartment and put them in Mike's garage for storage. Getting my clothing and shopping spree items into my two bags proved difficult, so I decided to just buy another suitcase.

I picked up my ringing phone. "Hello, sexy," I teased.

"Hey, you. What are you doing?"

"Just realizing I need another suitcase," I said, laughing.

"Do you want to do that and then meet me for lunch?"

"Sounds good. Where and when?"

"That diner we ate breakfast at last week. Call me when you are on your way."

"Okay, see you soon," I said. I grabbed my keys and headed out the door.

I called Mike as soon as I finished checking out at the luggage store. When I pulled into the parking lot and saw his truck, I felt a warm comfortable feeling wash over me. He gave me a nod as I pulled up beside him.

Our conversation was light until I remembered I was leaving the next day. The sadness hit me like a ton of bricks.

"Tia, what's wrong?"

"I just realized I leave tomorrow! I hate leaving days. They make me sad." I reached for his hand.

"Me too. We can't help but feel sad. But I know it will be okay. The sadness will go away in a few days."

"Well, I should get to the spa. I have my last meeting with Annie about the preparations for closing it down. I will handle everything else by phone and Skype. Please, can you give a hand with the vendors and equipment sales? I have listed reputable companies and will e-mail Clare to keep you informed."

"Of course, sweetie. I have a busy afternoon too. Will I see you tonight?"

"Yes, of course."

⋗⫯⟡⫯⟐⫯⟡⫯⟡⫯⟐⟡⫯⋖

Our last evening was impeccable. Mike wined and dined me, and then we made love in silence. We were as close as we had ever been. There were no tears, no promises, and no expectations. Once it was over, we were silent. We both knew the inevitable was upon us. Mike finally broke the silence.

"Well, I guess I better get going so you can get some sleep. Big day tomorrow." His lips were smiling, but his eyes were sad.

"Yeah, big day," I said sarcastically through pouty lips.

We held each other tight, and the sound of our hearts beating did the talking.

"Will you have time for a cup of coffee before your flight?"

"Yes, I would like that."

I kissed him softly and locked the door behind him.

⤗⤖ CONCLUSION ⤕⤔

*H*e smiled at me as I entered the airport coffee shop. "Good morning, beautiful."

Hmm, I thought, *how ironic. It will end as it began with a coffee cup in my hand.* "Not a good morning," I said aloud. "It's a travel day."

"Well, you look good for your travel day."

I smiled and handed him the short list I had worked on the night before.

"What's this?" he said, looking a little concerned.

"Don't worry. It's just a little something to let you know how much I love you."

He opened it up and looked at me.

"Just read it!"

"Okay, Miss Bossy." He smiled and began reading my words out loud.

> *Some of the little things I love about you …*
> *The way your polo shirts are snug on your biceps*
> *Your honest, round, beautiful, brown eyes*
> *Your strong jawline*
> *The way your pants fit your sexy round butt*
> *The way you take control and bring calm in situations*
> *when no one else can*
> *The way you make love to me*
> *How beautiful you make me feel*
> *Your kindness and generosity toward people*
> *Your laugh*
> *Your smile … God, I love your smile!*

When he was done reading, he halfway blushed and lowered his eyes for just a moment. "I love it. Thanks, Tia."

"Well, I guess I better get going. Don't want to miss my plane," I said, trying to hide my panic.

He walked with me to the security line. "Can't you stay just a while longer, please?" He looked like a sad little puppy.

"Mike, I can't! I have to get back to the girls, to my company," I said, trying to hold it together. But then the emotion hit me. "Mike, what if this is it?" I questioned, trying to hold back the tears. "How do I say good-bye to a love that awakened me as a woman?"

He held me tight. I could barely breathe, and I felt his body shaking as he held back his own emotion.

"I have been asking myself why—why did I fall in love with a woman who lives six thousand miles away from me? Oh god! I will miss you."

We kissed passionately for the last time, and as he held me in his arms, he whispered in my ear. "One day we will know, Tia. We don't know what the future will bring, but the dots will be connected. I promise." He smiled and gently touched my face.

"Bye, babe," I said, the only words I could get out.

"Tia, it is bye for *now*," he said, correcting me.

I turned to walk away and did not look back. I now trusted in myself.

"Aloha, ladies and gentlemen. We welcome you aboard Hawaiian Airlines flight 51 bound for Kahului, Maui."

I put in my earbuds and wiped a tear from my face.